ALF'S SECRET WAR

Donald Lightwood

CANONGATE · KELPIES

In fond memory of

May and Ethel . . .

First published in Great Britain in 1992
by Canongate Press Plc,
14 Frederick Street,
EDINBURGH EH2 2HB

ISBN 0 86241 383 4

The publishers acknowledge subsidy from
the Scottish Arts Council towards the
publication of this volume.

Phototypeset by Hewer Text Composition Services,
Edinburgh

Printed and bound in Great Britain by
Cox and Wyman, Reading

ALF'S SECRET WAR

1

Alf stared at the policeman standing on the opposite side of the stage. Like Alf, he was hidden from the audience and watching Alf's parents, Sonia and Dave, doing the first part of their act. Sonia was playing the ukulele and Dave was doing one of his 'daft dances' as he called them. In this one he was supposed to be an air-raid warden trying to put out a fire with a stirrup pump. Alf couldn't help noticing that, unlike the audience, the policeman didn't laugh at any of Dave's gags.

Sonia glanced off, checking that Alf was there, ready to come on stage. He gave her a thumbs up and she smiled back. Her face was wet with sweat. The full house and the lights made the stage very hot. Alf himself was boiling in the thick Royal Air Force uniform he had to wear. Fitting him out in one of the uniforms of the three services had been his dad's idea. It enabled them to cash in on the audience's strong feelings for the armed forces during the war. He was dressed as a Flight Sergeant because this week they were performing in Wolverhampton, near to the big RAF camp at Cosford. The family's act was known on the music hall circuit as *Sonia, Dave and Sonny — A Song, A Dance, And A Smile*. Alf hated the name Sonny, but he was lumbered with it because it sounded snappy. And he had to admit it looked good on the posters outside the theatres where they appeared.

There was a loud burst of laughter. Dave had got

his foot stuck in his bucket. For a first house they were a good audience. Of course it was Saturday night, and unless there was an air-raid, it was bound to go well. Alf took care not to let the butterflies in his belly make him nervous. What would have been an exciting experience for any other eleven year old boy was a job of work to him.

The applause died away for Dave's dance and he put on a serious voice as he began to speak his monologue 'Salute To The Boys In Blue' (elsewhere it would have been Khaki or Navy Blue). The band played 'There'll Always Be An England' very quietly behind his words, and the audience were still and silent, bound together by the comradeship of war. As Dave reached the climax of his recitation and the music started to swell, Alf noticed the policeman again. He was talking to the stage manager and pointing at his father, just as Dave's final words were echoing round the theatre. '. . . God bless the Boys in Blue!'

And then Alf saw his mother waving for him to come on. He'd missed his cue! He panicked and marched quickly on to the stage as the band played a fanfare. He halted beside his father and saluted. The audience, many of them in RAF uniform themselves, cheered Alf as he stood smartly to attention in the centre of the stage.

Dave put on an officer's cap and Alf brought his arm down from the salute.

'And what's your name Airman?' asked Dave.

'Flight Sergeant Bulldog sir,' replied Alf. The audience laughed. As they did when he was Petty Officer Bulldog in Plymouth, or Colour Sergeant Bulldog in Aldershot.

'Tell me Bulldog, where are you stationed?' Dave asked in his posh officer's voice.

'Oh, a smashing little place sir. Just like home from home.'

'You are a lucky chap,' said Dave. 'Where's that?'

Dave had taught Alf that his reply to this question was the best line in the act. Simply mentioning the name of the local barracks or camp was a sure-fire winner. For some reason Alf couldn't understand, the audience were bound to shout and cheer when he named the local base.

'Cosford sir.'

The audience went wild. During this exchange, Sonia had popped off the stage. She now came back wearing an RAF cap and carrying a parcel. 'Sir, sir. The Flight Sergeant's secret weapon has just arrived.' Sonia handed the parcel to Alf.

Dave put on an overdone look of astonishment. 'What's this? I don't know anything about a secret weapon.' Alf undid his parcel and took out a cricket bat. Dave examined it and exclaimed, 'A cricket bat! What are you going to do with that?'

Alf swung his bat. 'Knock old Hitler for six, sir!'

The three of them lined up for their final number as everyone in the theatre shouted their approval.

Dave looked down into the orchestra pit and spoke to the band. 'Gentlemen, are you ready? After three. Here we go . . . Three!'

The band struck up and Sonia, Dave and Sonny launched into the song they had made popular throughout the country.

> We're going to Hit Hit Hitler
> Where it Hurt Hurt Hurts.
> We're going to Knock Knock Knock
> Him on the Head Head Head.
> Watch out Adolf 'olf 'olf
> We're on our Way Way Way
> What'll you Say Say Say
> When you're Dead Dead DEAD!

'That was the best first house we've ever had,' said

Sonia, after they had taken their final bow and left the stage.

'You can say that again,' said Dave. 'Right me old cock sparrow?' he added to Alf.

'Not 'alf guvnor,' replied Alf.

Laughing they reached their dressing-room.

There was a policeman standing by the door. He spoke to Dave. 'Mr Dugmore? Mr David Dugmore?'

Dave and Sonia halted abruptly. Their happy faces changed in an instant. When Dave replied his voice was hoarse. 'What if I am?'

The policeman took a buff envelope from his pocket. 'I'm here to give you this.' Dave took the letter and the policeman regarded him scornfully. 'It seems you bin careless with your post, Mr Dugmore. Like not opening it and that. Now the authorities have tracked you down and I've bin told to make sure you get this. *And* open it. *And* read it.'

Dave sighed. 'There's no need to make a song and dance about it.'

The policeman responded swiftly. 'Don't you come the smart-alec with me. *I'm* doing my duty. Unlike some I could mention . . .'

The man's heavy-handed sarcasm and attitude to his dad upset Alf. He'd never heard anyone talk like that to him before. He tried to get Dave's attention.

Dave ignored Alf and looked at his wife. She spoke to him. 'It had to happen sooner or later, Dave.' She put her arm around Alf and held him to her. He could feel her trembling and it affected him. What was it? What was going on?

The constable spoke to Dave. 'You got to open it.'

'I know what's in it.'

'I'll bet you do,' he replied with a sneer.

Sonia bridled. 'Don't you take that tone of voice.'

'I'll take any tone I like when I'm talking to his sort,' replied the policeman, indicating Dave with his thumb. '*And* you, come to that,' he added to Sonia. 'I s'pose you didn't know he was dodging his call-up?' He answered himself. 'Not half you didn't.'

'You don't know anything about it,' said Sonia.

The policeman laughed in her face. 'That's what you think. I'll just tell you what I *do* know. I know they bin chasing him round the country with his call-up. And I know he's received the letters, *and* I know he's destroyed them. D'you want to see the list of landladies we've spoke to?' Sonia remained silent and Alf felt her hand tighten on his shoulder. The constable's pomposity grew as he went on. 'Think of the time he's caused us to waste. Time we could've spent on the war effort. Did that worry him? Not on your life. That's the way with cowards. They only think of themselves.'

Alf threw himself at the policeman. He grabbed the man's belt and hung on, kicking as hard as he could. Sonia shouted at Alf, and then screamed as the policeman clouted her son's head. Striking at the constable with one hand, she tugged at Alf with the other. With a great heave, the man thrust the two from him and they stumbled to the floor. Dave swore and squared up to the policeman, who was now pulling out his truncheon.

'No Dave!' shouted Sonia. She clung on to his leg, holding him back. 'Don't, it'll only make things worse for you.' Dave hesitated, giving Sonia time to get up and put her arms around him. 'Never mind, love. Never mind. It'll be all right, you'll see.'

The constable spoke to Dave. 'I'm warning you . . .'

Alf scrambled up, his head still dizzy from the blow he'd received. 'You leave my dad alone.'

'And you stay where you are,' said the policeman, pointing his truncheon at Alf. 'Assaulting a police officer is a serious offence.'

'He's only a kid,' said Sonia. 'Lay off him.'

The policeman addressed Sonia. 'I'm telling you here and now to control this child. Responsible parents would've tanned his hide for what he's done here tonight.'

Sonia opened the dressing-room door and bundled Alf inside. He protested. 'Do as I say,' she said firmly and shut the door.

Automatically Alf went to his chair at his part of the long dressing-table. He stood holding the back of the chair and feeling numb all over. The murmur of voices continued outside, but he couldn't hear what they were saying. His head was throbbing.

He became aware of tears trickling down his face. He was appalled. Had he been crying out there? He wiped his eyes roughly. As he did so, he tried hard not to remember. But it was impossible. The harder he tried, the clearer his memory became. The word had lodged in his head and it wouldn't be moved. Coward.

He knew the word very well. Everybody knew the Italians were cowards. Lots of comedians they worked with told jokes about the cowardly Eyeties. But it was daft to say his dad was like that, because he wasn't.

Alf found himself thinking about his Uncle Bill, his dad's brother. He was in the army and they had seen him on his last leave. Alf had been very impressed with his uncle's cigarette lighter that had been made out of old cartridge case. His uncle had joked about what his dad was missing, not being in the army. Alf remembered his dad's funny answer. He'd said *he* was minding *his* business, why couldn't Bill do the same? Uncle Bill had left pretty soon after that. And they hadn't gone to the pub together.

Without wanting to, Alf heard the policeman's voice outside. It wasn't fair. Why did he have to come and spoil everything? Just when it was smashing. Reflected in the dressing-table mirror he saw their props basket. On top of it was the army cap his dad sometimes used in the act.

Everything in the mirror blurred — the cap, the

basket, his face. This time he knew he was crying and he let the tears come. He pressed one into his cheek and rubbed hard. His tears brought thoughts of rotten things. For no reason at all, he pictured the digs they were living in that week. He saw the grate in which the landlady would not light a fire. The linoleum curling in his bedroom; the bed, cold and lumpy. The whole house cheerless, like so many of the boarding houses that were his home. The three of them continually made jokes about the awful places they ended up in. Especially his dad. Alf remembered how he and his mom had hugged each other, laughing at some crack from Dave. Sometimes he would do an impersonation of the landlady, toothless and heaving her bosom like a pantomime dame. Even now a smile forced its way through his tears. His dad was great. Smashing. He didn't care what they said about him.

The door opened and Sonia and Dave came in. Sonia saw Alf's tears and immediately set about drying them with her hankie. 'What did you go and do that for? We'd got enough trouble as it was.'

'Dad, have you got to go in the army?'

'It looks like it son.' Dave forced a grin. 'It seems they can't do without me.'

'Should you have gone before?'

Dave and Sonia glanced at each other. Dave kicked off his shoes and started to remove his stage clothes. Sonia pulled her chair close to Alf and sat down beside him. 'Dad thought it would be best if we stuck together. We're a good team.'

'But *should* you have gone Dad?'

'Well, sort of. After my medical they gave me a period of time to get things sorted out. I just extended it a bit.' Dave peeled off his shirt.

Alf stared at his dad. 'So you should have.'

Again Sonia answered. 'Like I said, dad had to think of us and the act.'

Alf turned on her. 'But he *should* have. It's the

11

law. I've seen it in the papers. They can put you in prison.'

'You sound as if you wanted me off in the army,' said Dave.

Alf struggled with his reply. 'I *don't* want you to go. But you *should* have. Like Uncle Bill.'

Dave gave a false laugh. 'Sounds like double Dutch to me.'

'Alf, why don't you go and see if Bert's got the fish and chips yet,' said Sonia. She smoothed his hair. Alf pulled his head away. He knew very well she was changing the subject.

'He'll bring them up,' said Alf. 'Like he has every other night,' he added, indicating he knew what she was up to.

'In that case you can clean off your make-up,' replied his mother. 'Your face is a mess. We'll need to do it again for the second house.'

Alf got up and moved away. He stood by the props hamper and picked at it. Sonia turned to the mirror and fiddled with her hair. Dave put cream on his face and started to remove his make-up. The room was silent. For a few minutes each was alone with their thoughts.

'Dad, are you scared of fighting the Germans?'

Sonia spoke to Alf with a strained voice. 'Will you listen to me, your father . . .'

Dave interrupted.'Let me speak to him.' He tossed aside his make-up towel and sat on the hamper beside Alf. The wickerwork creaked and Dave brushed towel fluff from his stubble. The familiar sweet smell of removing cream filled the dressing-room. 'Yes, I *am* scared son. But it's not the Germans. I'm scared of leaving you and mom. Can you understand that? I don't want to go away because I love you.' Alf fiddled with a piece of loose wicker. He heard his mother looking for her hankie. 'We've got something special, you and Mom and me. We're on the way up in the business. What a waste, to break that up.'

The silence returned to the room. Dave gently put his arm around his son. Alf stayed still. Then he mumbled. 'That policeman said you are a coward.'

His father sighed and squeezed Alf's arm. 'What does he know about anything?'

'Because you didn't go off to the war. When you should.'

Sonia spoke angrily to Alf. 'Stop it. You're too young to understand. Dad's tried to explain. That's that.'

'Leave him be love,' said Dave. He steered Alf to his chair. 'Come on. Clean your face up.'

There was a knock on the door and Bert the call-boy walked in. Sonia turned her anger on him. 'I've told you before, you don't just walk in here.'

Bert paid no attention and dropped a greasy newspaper packet on the table. 'No fish, only chips. I got you a tanner's worth each.'

'No fish. That's the limit,' said Sonia.

Bert spoke to her cheekily. 'There's a war on — didn't you know?'

'I'll drop one on you, one of these days,' said Dave, giving the boy one-and-sixpence.

'They'm saying downstairs the coppers come to tek you off,' said Bert. Dave pushed him out. 'What you bin doin' then, robbin' a bank?' He laughed as he just managed to avoid Dave's clout round his ear.

Dave shut the door. 'They might as well have put it in the nine o'clock news.' He handed round the packets of chips. Usually this was a happy time of day, relaxing and eating their supper between the houses. Tonight they ate in silence.

Sonia made a pot of tea. She turned off the small gas ring and poured the boiling water into the pot. She held the empty kettle suspended, as though she had forgotten it. The implications of what was to

13

happen to them were becoming more real by the minute. After tomorrow, Sunday, there would be no more Dave. He had to report to Colchester at eight o'clock on Monday morning. She would be left with Alf and she would still have to earn a living. Dave took the kettle from her and put it down. They faced each other, saying nothing.

Like most children, Alf became embarrassed when his parents showed tenderness towards each other. He was overcome by red-faced awkwardness when they kissed, or held each other. They never thought of *him* on these occasions, and how he had to suffer. In the mirror he saw his father put his arms round his mother, who rested her head on his shoulder. Guiltily Alf looked away from the reflection. He heard his mother sob.

Having cleaned his face, there was nothing left to do but put on fresh make-up. He put stripes on his face with a stubby stick of pink greasepaint. It didn't matter how you did this, since it all had to be rubbed together to make a foundation. You could make yourself look like a Red Indian, or write your name — anything, so long as you got enough on your face. It didn't occur to Alf to play around with the foundation stick now. He simply ran the lines up and down his face. When he'd been making-up for the first house, he'd added a few horizontal lines and played noughts and crosses. He put a touch of cream on his fingers and rubbed the pink all over his face. It was at this point that his mother usually helped him. Since she was clearly too upset, Alf decided to finish the job himself. He put a spot of red on each cheek, and a dab on his chin. He never understood the bit on his chin. But his mother said it helped to give his face 'shape'. He rubbed the red in and worked away at the hard edges where it joined the pink. Next a touch of blue eye shadow. This was more difficult — badly applied it could make you look as though you'd got a

14

black eye. However, he was satisfied with the effect he created. The eyebrow pencil called for a steady hand. He managed quite nicely, with only a couple of slips. He couldn't remember how his mother did the line round his eyelashes, so he used the eyebrow pencil for that as well. Finally some carmine on his lips. This necessitated a little guessing, because the pink foundation made it difficult to see their shape. To fix the make-up, he powdered his face with blending powder.

It must have been the cloud of powder that reawakened his parents to his presence. As though *they* now felt guilty, they separated and, one on each side, they joined him at the dressing table. The three looked into the mirror. Alf knew he had got his make-up wrong. He looked like some kind of clown. So he laughed. And they laughed. But after a few moments he saw they were also crying. Tears were streaming down their faces. Even his dad. They put their arms around him and hugged him. He felt their tears on his own face. Alf had never seen a man cry before.

He wriggled free and buried his head in his arms. 'Stop it! Stop it!' He shouted into his arms.

They let him go. But it wasn't their loving hug that had made him burst out. It was the sight of his dad crying. Something he'd never expected to see in a million years.

2

Alf didn't have to go to school on Monday morning. This was the only crumb of comfort left to him. On Sunday he and Sonia had seen Dave off at the station at Wolverhampton. They had then travelled on to Birmingham, where they were booked to perform at the Hippodrome. It had been awful. His mom and dad had clung to each other until the last moment. And his mom cried on the train.

Sonia and Alf were waiting to see the manager at the Hippodrome. They were sitting in the circle bar, the walls of which were covered with pictures of well-known performers. Alf felt like throwing mud at their brightly coloured smiles. Why should *they* be happy? He whispered to Sonia. 'Mom, what are we going to *do*?'

'I told you in the digs,' she replied irritably. 'I'll do the first solo spot. And then we'll do the second same as usual, except I'll do a number, instead of dad's dance. You'll just come on, the same as always.'

'But what about dad's . . .'

'I'll do dad's part. It'll be all right. We'll rehearse it this afternoon.'

Sonia left Alf behind when she was called in to the manager's office. He wandered round the bar and pulled faces at the grinning photographs. The place smelt of stale smoke and drink. He acted being sick and reeled into the auditorium. He found himself at the back of the dress circle. The band-call was taking place. This was when the performers explained to the

16

musical director how they wanted their music played. Each act had to provide band parts and the MD would run through anything they were not familiar with.

'You on this week?' An elderly cleaner had appeared beside Alf. He nodded. 'Got any fags?'

'What? Oh, no.'

'They've run out again. Blinkin' shops.' She started looking in the ashtrays on the back of the seats. 'Y'can sometimes pick up a good nub-end, if you're lucky.'

A splatter of applause came from the band as a large woman strolled on to the stage. The cleaner nudged Alf. 'Two Ton Tessie,' she said. 'Top o' the bill.'

Tessie O'Shea was extremely popular. She was fat and jovial, with a talent for making fun of her size. Audiences loved the comic songs she performed with her ukulele. She handed her music to the MD. 'My usual,' was all she said. And then added: 'But just play the right notes this time, for a change.' The band laughed and she ambled off.

'Her's a real pro,' said the cleaner. 'Always packs 'em in her does.'

Dave had normally attended to their Monday morning band-calls. Seeing what went on for the first time, Alf realised how unfair life was. *He'd* be stuck in another rotten school, while his dad just waltzed along to the theatre to hand in their dots. To hear Dave go on about it, you'd have thought he'd had to personally rehearse the band for hours.

He returned to find Sonia coming out of the manager's office with tight lips. She took Alf by the arm and marched him down the stairs. Sonia halted at the bottom. 'Do you know when I'm to go on for my solo spot? First. After the overture, me — the first act!' She continued angrily, 'I told him I'd never been so insulted. All he could say was we'd let him down.'

'We have though, haven't we? Without dad?'

'That's not *our* fault. I asked him if he knew there was a war on. He didn't like that. Think of it. I've been

17

in the business for ten years, and they bung me at the bottom of the bill.'

Sonia had been a solo performer before she got married. However, Alf knew their present act depended on Dave. Of course he couldn't say that to her. So he told her about Tessie O'Shea.

His mother reacted. 'Don't tell me. I know. Talk about luck. This week of all weeks, who have they got top of the bill? Only the best female uke act in the country.'

Alf remained silent. With their normal act it wouldn't have mattered. For the most part Sonia only supported Dave, playing the ukulele for his songs and dances. A horrible fear began to take hold of Alf. *It wouldn't work*. Whatever Sonia did in her solo spot. And he was sure she felt the same.

They made their way backstage. Once through the stagedoor they had to weave their way past hampers and props. These belonged to the current week's acts and a number of fellow performers were trying to sort out their belongings.

'Sonia! Sonia, my love!' An over made-up woman rushed towards them. This was Yolanda, Mistress of Illusion, as she was styled on the posters. She kissed Sonia on each cheek and tried to do the same to Alf. He craftily avoided her large lipsticked mouth and gave her a wave instead. 'I've just heard about Dave. Oh, what a misery for you. What on earth will you do?'

'Carry on,' replied Sonia briefly.

'Dave was *so* good.'

'I know.'

'Everybody said so. *So* original. By the way, have you seen who's top of the bill?'

Sonia sent Alf to check the arrival of their hamper from the station. He moved away from the women thankfully — Yolanda's perfume would give anybody a headache. He found their hamper and undid the

18

straps. His dad's stuff was on top. Alf picked up the army cap Dave had used in the act. If his dad had been here, like before, he might never have found out about him. He could have grown up never knowing he was a coward. Alf put the cap on. It flopped down over his ears. Dave would have a real one by now.

The cap was snatched from his head. It was Sonia. She threw the cap in the hamper and slammed the lid. 'She's a cat. Loving it she was. Rubbing my nose in it. She just loved that.'

'What?' asked Alf.

'It's obvious, isn't it? Me being dropped in it. The cat.'

'Mom, would it be any good if I came on with you? For your first spot?'

Sonia's bitterness prevented her from seeing that this was the only way Alf could think of helping her. She snapped at him. 'Don't be daft.'

'Couldn't it help?'

'How? We've got nothing we could do. No band parts. Nothing. This isn't the Women's Institute you know. They're not going to go oo and ah just because *you* walk on. This is a number one booking. They're used to classy acts.' Sonia empted a carrier bag of sheet music on to the hamper. 'No. There's nothing else for it. I've got to do some of my old speciality numbers.' She sorted through the songs. Alf hadn't heard of half of them. They must have been ancient.

Alf watched his mother place the music in piles. He wanted to tell her he would do anything to help her. But he couldn't tell her, because he couldn't think what the anything might be. *She* would have to tell *him*. And he knew she was in no mood to do that.

The stage manager shouted down the corridor. 'Sonia and Sonny? They here? The MD's waiting.'

Sonia left Alf and went to attend to the band-call. He sat down on their hamper. From nearby he heard the sound of cooing coming from an oblong basket.

He investigated. They were white doves and obviously part of Yolanda's magic act. He had seen a number of these acts from the wings. It intrigued him to see how the magicians cheated the audience by hiding rabbits and doves. Of course he knew they had secret pockets. But he still didn't understand how you could hide a real live bird in one. He put his finger through one of the air holes in the basket. A dove nibbled it so gently he could hardly feel anything. He stroked the bird's neck. It cooed at him.

The idea to take the dove out was stupid. He knew that, even as he was opening the basket. But he did it nevertheless. He had absolutely no right to mess with other people's property. However, the pleasure he got holding the dove made the risk worthwhile. It calmed his fear and he would be very careful.

Having no secret pockets, nor indeed any pocket large enough, Alf tucked the dove inside his jacket. It created a large bulge and left him wondering how a secret pocket could be contrived to make a bird smaller. And yet it must. You never saw tell-tale lumps like this in stage magicians' clothes. He contented himself with holding the bulge in place and enjoying the amazing amount of warmth generated by the dove. After a while there was a sudden increase in heat, just above his waist, roughly where the bird's tail was. This new spot of heat also felt damp.

Alf opened his jacket and took the dove out. He was horrified. There was a sloppy white mess on his pullover. He quickly put the bird down and looked for something to clean himself up with. The dove took a few steps along the hamper and then flew off. Alf froze. It flew down the corridor. He ran after the bird, almost colliding with the stage manager, who was coming in the opposite direction.

'Is that one of Yolanda's birds?' asked the man. Alf nodded. 'What are you doing with it?'

'Er, looking after it,' replied Alf.

'Well, you're not doing a very good job, are you?'

The stage manager went on his way and Alf rushed down the corridor. This was where the star performers had their dressing-rooms, close to the stage. He'd lost sight of the dove. The swing doors at the end of the corridor were closed. However, one of the dressing-room doors was open. Alf tiptoed to it and looked in. He saw Tessie O'Shea holding the dove in her hands.

'Are you looking for this lovely little lady, or fellow, or whatever it might be?'

'Yes. It flew away.'

'That's birds all over for you.' She carefully handed the dove back to Alf, who made a point of holding it away from himself. 'You'll be with the magic act?'

'No, I'm with my mother. She's doing the band-call We're Sonia and Sonny.'

'So you'll be Sonny. What do you do Sonny?'

'Sing songs and mom plays . . .' He hesitated, and then plunged in. 'She plays the ukulele. Same as you.'

This time Tessie hesitated. She raised her eyebrows. 'I see. Well, fancy that.'

He told her about Dave's having to leave the act and the situation they were in. With Sonia having to go solo, and both of them worried. Tessie listened sympathetically and Alf was sure he'd found a friend.

'That's bad luck.' She noticed Alf's pullover. 'Don't tell me that innocent little thing you're holding did that to you?' She reprimanded the dove. 'You are a disgrace, so you are. Let's see if we can do something about that.' She guided him to the washhand basin and sponged the mess away. 'You can tell your mother you spilt your pop.'

Alf smiled. He really liked this large woman. 'Miss O'Shea, could I ask you something?'

'I should think so, Sonny.'

'I've had this idea. Could *you* help my mother?'

21

'How? By doing your laundry?' She gave a loud laugh.

'I mean with her act. Her solo spot — with the uke and that.'

Tessie held up her hand. 'Whoa there. I don't think your mother would be very pleased if I started butting in. You know the music hall. It's not done, is it, interfering with somebody's act?'

'Just to help her. She hasn't done it for years and I know she's worried. I don't know what to do. Couldn't you help her, just this once?'

Tessie looked at Alf as he stood clutching the dove. She touched the bird's head. 'You know something bird — this here's a good son.' She then spoke to Alf. 'I'll tell you what I'll do. I'll watch her during the first house. If things seem okay, I could maybe have a chat with her between the houses. I'm not promising anything mind.'

'You won't tell her I said anything, will you?'

Tessie shook her head. 'It'll be our secret, me ould darlin'. Toodlepip.'

'Thank you,' said Alf. 'Thank you ever so much.

'Your father's been called-up then?'

'Yes.'

The landlady was setting the tea table with thick white china. 'How's he manage to keep out so long?'

'. . . He was sick.'

'And him on the halls?'

'He had to keep taking these pills. Six times a day. For ever such a long time. Till he got better.' Alf prayed she wouldn't ask any more questions.

She didn't. She had stopped still, holding a bottle of sauce. 'My hubby was in the army. I lost him. He was killed last year. At El Alamein.'

Embarrassed, Alf mumbled he was sorry. The landlady went on. 'All that way from home. North Africa. No grave. Nothing. What's it all for? That's what I ask myself.' She stopped speaking and there was an uncomfortable silence.

'To beat Hitler,' he said, not realising she was not really looking for an answer.

She banged the bottle down on the table. 'Let me tell you, there's some here in this country every bit as bad as Hitler. D'you think them posh MPs have to put up with it like ordinary people? Not on your life. Why aren't *they* called up? You don't see none of them in the desert. We're all supposed to do our bit. That's what they tell us. Sitting on their fat backsides, that's all they do. That's *their* bit.'

The sound of Sonia's ukulele came from upstairs. She had been practising all afternoon; first with Alf, and now by herself.

'They're special though,' said Alf.

'Who says so?'

'They're the government.'

'And because of that, *they* don't get killed.'

Alf had never heard anyone speak like this before. He was sure everybody believed in the war effort and knew that one day we would win. He could see how she would be sad because of her husband. But going on about the government was daft. They were winning the war for us.

'What about Mr Churchill?' He flung this question at her, convinced that even she could not object to the Prime Minister.

'Him, what's he ever done for the working man?'

'He's winning the war. Everybody says so. It's in the papers.'

The landlady sneered. Alf was shocked. 'He's not doing it for the working man. He's doing it so his lot can keep what they got when it's over.'

He really had no idea what she was talking about. His impression of the war at the front was drawn from the newsreels he saw at the cinema and the news he heard on the wireless. It was exciting, the fighting and winning battles. And there were the stories in his comic. Of course he knew they were just stories. But they made you feel as though you were there, killing Germans and capturing things.

'Your father could be killed. Then what would you think of it?'

Alf caught his breath. To hear said out loud what you shouldn't even think, stunned him. He saw no link between the fighting and people he knew. His Uncle Bill had been in the army a long time, but he'd never imagined him being in a battle. You just didn't. As for his dad. Whatever he'd thought about him over the last couple of days, he'd never thought about him being killed.

'He won't be,' said Alf defiantly.

'That's what I said about Jack.'

Alf left the room and went outside to the yard. He went into the lavatory next to the coal shed and locked the door. It was the only place he could think of going where he'd be safe from the landlady. There were neat squares of newspaper hanging on a nail. He flicked through them to see if there were any pictures of tanks or planes. There was nothing, so he made one of the pieces of paper into a dart. There was a gap of about six inches between the top of the door and the frame. He decided to aim his dart at that. If it went through, everything would be all right. His dad would not be killed and the act would be okay. He launched the dart and it went clean through. His spirits lifted and he shouted a silent Yippee. To make this good omen even better, he took his piece of lucky shrapnel out of his pocket. Travelling around, he'd not been able to gather a good collection of shrapnel like most boys. So he'd made his one and only piece special. It was part of an anti-aircraft shell that had brought down a German bomber, when he'd been in Coventry. At least, that was what he told himself. He held the shrapnel hard and wished. That done, he hoped he hadn't mysteriously weakened the good omen of the dart. You never knew with stuff like that.

His mother was sitting at the table when he got back into the house. She told him to wash his hands and he edged past the landlady into the back kitchen. She was taking their tea through. He heard her start droning on to Sonia. Alf was sure the woman was mad. He'd never met a mad person and he was disappointed it was not more exciting. Maybe one day she would become a proper lunatic and have to be restrained.

She was still carrying on with her crazy talk when he sat down at the table.

'D'you think the workers in Germany wanted this war? Course not. No more than we did here. Did *you*?' Sonia shook her head. 'See? Course you didn't. Neither did me and Jack. And there he is — dead and gone.' She stared into space. 'It's criminal. And there's him at the paper shop. They haven't taken *him*. He's not sick or nothing, like your hubby was.' Muttering to herself she left the room.

Sonia and Alf chewed their dried egg on toast.

'Did you tell her dad was sick?' she asked him and he nodded. 'That was sensible. We'd better stick to that.'

'She's mad,' said Alf.

'Well, she has lost her husband, poor woman.'

'And she doesn't know anything about the war,' he added.

The audience at the Hippodrome lived up to the reputation of Monday first house audiences everywhere. They were grim and their response was luke-warm. Sonia's solo spot won a few half-hearted claps.

'Thanks for warming them up dear,' said Yolanda, who was waiting to go on.

Her catty remark was lost on Sonia, who brushed past Alf and rushed to the dressing-room. He followed her. However, when he heard her sobbing inside, he decided to wait before he went in. He made his way back to the stage to watch Yolanda.

He met Tessie in the corridor.

'Hullo Sonny. I saw your mum. What an audience! Ask her if she'd like to pop in and have a cup of tea with me between houses.' She winked at him. 'Is that your dove on stage now? I hope he behaves himself!'

Alf ran back to the dressing-room. His mother was sitting stiffly in a chair. 'Mom, Mom . . .'

'Not now Alf,' she said.

'But Mom . . .'

She looked at Alf and her face silenced him. She was biting her teeth together and shivering. To Alf the impression was that she was so upset, she was ill.

'Are you all right Mom?'

'Just leave me be.'

He sat at his dressing-table. He was already made up, so there was nothing to do. He looked in the mirror at some of the notices stuck on the wall behind him. He tried to read them, but it was impossible. He couldn't work out why mirrors always turned letters round the wrong way.

There was a sharp knock on the door. The manager came in. Sonia stood up and faced him, as though she had been expecting his visit.

'I'm sorry Sonia, but it won't work out,' he told her.

'What do you mean?'

'I said I'd give you a try first house. Well, it won't work.'

She took a step towards him. 'Come on now, you don't know what I had to put up with out there.'

The manager waved her words away. 'I know about the house.'

'Just let me finish, will you. I only had to do the whole of my spot with that woman watching me from the side. Tessie O'Shea. How would *you* feel? What's she need to be there for anyway?'

26

The manager shrugged his shoulders. 'It's a free country.'

'Oh, come on . . .'

'All right then, she plays the uke. She probably wanted to size up the competition.'

Alf interrupted. 'But Mom . . .' Sonia turned on him angrily and told him to be quiet.

'Anyway, it doesn't make any difference,' continued the manager. 'I never should have let you on in the first place. Two uke acts — it's madness. I let my feelings get the better of me. I was sorry for you, losing Dave. But it won't work. Just pack up your stuff and let's call it a day. Here's a couple of quid to cover you for your first spot. I'm sorry Sonia. But there it is.'

'So that's it. No second spot?'

'There's no point.' He looked at her squarely. 'Is there?'

'I've never been so insulted . . .'

'Forget it love. I had a contract with *Sonia, Dave and Sonny*, remember? You broke it.' He carried on over her objection. 'Don't go on. If I wanted to be nasty, I could have Dave for breach of contract.'

'He couldn't help being called-up.'

'He'd have had a few weeks' notice of an ordinary call-up. I wasn't born yesterday. I know the game he was playing. You know as well as me, he had no right to sign a contract.' The manager went to the door. 'I could have him prosecuted if I wanted. So don't give me any fuss. All right?' He left the room.

Sonia remained standing, looking at the door. 'I'll never forgive that woman. Never.'

Alf spoke. 'Does that mean we're not going to go on in the second half?'

'You heard what he said. We're finished.' She sat down wearily. 'I would have been fine. I know I would. Three of my old numbers. I had them all worked out. And I started great. Then I saw her, standing there in the wings. I couldn't believe it. I thought I was going to lose my voice. And my fingers. I played the uke like I'd got gloves on. How could she? I always thought she was a top professional. How could she be so mean?'

Alf began to realise the enormity of the mistake he'd made. He should have *known*. 'Mom, listen. She wasn't being mean.'

'Of course she was.'

'No, honest. She wanted to help you.'

'Don't be ridiculous.'

'I *know* she did. She said she'd have a talk with you between the houses.' How could he have been so stupid? How? If only he'd thought. If only he hadn't opened that basket; taken the dove out. If only he hadn't chased after it. If only . . .

'She what? She spoke to you?'

Alf told his mother what he'd done, and set the seal on the worst three days of his life.

3

Sonia and Alf went to live with Dave's mother, Granny Dugmore, in Smethwick. In spite of pleading phone calls, Sonia had been unable to prevent the cancellation of all their remaining bookings. Now that *Sonia, Dave and Sonny* were reduced to an untried duo, managers were not prepared to take a risk on them.

In fact Alf found that he enjoyed living at his gran's. This was mainly due to Grandad Charlie, his gran's brother, who had been bombed out and now lived with her. Alf had never known his Grandad Dugmore, who had died before he was born. So Charlie had stepped in and they got on very well. Because the house was so small, they had to share a bedroom and this led to long chats together. Alf told Charlie about the music hall stars he'd met. And Charlie would reminisce about the Boer War, which, according to him, might not have been won if he hadn't been there. Equally fascinating to Alf was the discovery that Charlie talked in his sleep. He'd experimented with talking back to the sleeping Charlie, and had succeeded in getting some half-sensible replies. He'd also discovered that he could get him to stop simply by telling him to *Shut Up Charlie*. This proved to be valuable on the nights when Charlie had been to the pub.

What was not so good about living in Smethwick was the boring routine of having to go on errands. He was also expected to look happy doing things he didn't like. This he could never work out. If you *did* look happy when you weren't — you were telling a lie. And the very people who told him to look happy were also the ones who told him it was a sin to lie. So where did that leave anybody?

These thoughts were going through his mind as he stood in the queue outside the butcher's. 'Oo, look!' said somebody and the queue surged towards the shop window. Word had got round that there was going to be some off-the-ration offal on sale. Alf got banged with shopping bags and his feet were trodden on. He couldn't understand what the fuss was about. All you could see in the shop was a bloody heap on the butcher's block. No attempt had been made to display the offal. It might still be lying on the slaughterhouse floor. Not that anyone minded. They just wanted to get their hands on some of it. The pushing continued and Alf began to fight back. He thrust his elbows out into the heaving bodies. Nobody seemed to notice, so he tried a few punches. But the women's bodies were so well-armoured with corsets and overcoats he made no impression.

A new tactic was required. As an inventor of secret weapons that would end the war, he knew he'd come up with something. A stink bomb would have been perfect, but he didn't have one. Anyway, it would have to be something more crafty than that.

He fainted. Or so the queue thought. Wisely he staged his fall so that he fell away from the jostling women and so avoided being trampled on. Immediately the queue broke up and formed a circle round him. To Alf's great satisfaction a woman screamed. Someone loosened his collar and tie, and he was carried into the shop. The butcher found a chair and they propped him up. He was given some cold tea to drink. It had saccharine in, which Alf hated, so he spat it out, pretending he couldn't swallow.

'The poor thing, he looks half-starved,' clucked one of the customers.

'Look, his eyes are opening.'

'He's trying to say something.'

Alf paused for effect, and then spoke in a whisper.

'What's he say?'

'Give him some air, can't you?' retorted the butcher. 'Now son, what is it? You tell me.' Bravely, Alf tried to sit up. The butcher held him. 'Just you tek it easy.'

With a great effort, Alf managed to speak. '. . . I've got to get my granny's offal.'

A sympathetic chorus came from the crowd. 'The brave little chap,' said somebody, to general approval.

'Don't worry yourself about that,' said the butcher. 'You sit there till you feel better.' He spoke to his assistant. 'Arthur, do him up some liver and kidneys. And chuck in a bit of heart an' all.'

The chorus of customers changed their tune to one of envy.

'Oo, I don't half feel ill!' said one.

'I'm going to pass out any minute!' added another.

The butcher laughed, humouring them. 'Oh ar? You'd better get off down Dudley Road Hospital then.' He placed a large newspaper parcel on Alf's lap. When Alf tried to pay him, he waved the money away. However, in a suitably weak voice, Alf had to insist on paying. His gran would have murdered him if she thought he'd wangled something for nothing.

The queue re-formed. After what he calculated to be the right length of time for his recovery, Alf thanked the butcher and left the shop. As he walked slowly past the queue, he was given the odd sweet and threepenny bit. When they were out of sight he broke into a run and shouted his current war-cry. Unfortunately his triumph was marred by a pain in his knee. He'd knocked off an old scab when he'd staged his fall and the wound was bleeding again. Like all boys his age, he was condemned to wear short trousers and his knees were perpetually in the wars. However, he didn't stop to clean himself up. Rather than waste the blood and pain, he put it to good use. He altered his stride and became a wounded warrior, valiantly returning home from the battle.

'Liver and kidney, *and* some 'eart! Strewth!' Grandad Charlie hugged Alf and danced him round the kitchen. 'This'll be worth putting my teeth in for.'

'If you can find them,' said Granny Dugmore. 'I bet you didn't do as well as our Alf. What did you get at the greengrocer's?'

'Some spuds and a few carrots,' Charlie replied.

'No onions?' He shook his head. 'Oh well, that'll have to do.' She spoke to Sonia, who was sitting apart, reading the *Birmingham Mail*. 'Come and give us an 'and Sonia.'

Sonia looked up. 'Where's the King's Highway?'

'Up Quinton, in' it Glad?' said Charlie.

Granny Dugmore nodded. 'It's that big public house.' She peeled the paper from the offal.

'What's going on up there, then?' Charlie asked Sonia.

'They're looking for a vocalist. For the band.'

'You don't want to go working in a place like that Sonia.' Granny Dugmore screwed up the bloody newspaper and threw it in the fire.

'I've got to get a job Gran,' replied Sonia.

'Not in one of them places,' she said firmly.

Sonia laughed. 'I can't be choosy. Especially around here. People aren't exactly falling over themselves to employ entertainers.'

Granny Dugmore responded impatiently. 'I've told you before, you could get a proper job if you put your mind to it. They'm crying out for women at Nettlefolds.'

'Sonia don't want to go working there Glad,' said

Charlie. 'Her's got talent, like our Dave. Be daft to waste it. Right Alf?'

'Right mate!' replied Alf, playing up. 'A song, a dance, and a smile — as seen by the Prince of Wales.'

'See!' Charlie laughed. 'Just you listen to the offal king!'

'Are you going to try for it Mom?'asked Alf.

Sonia knew that her mother-in-law would disapprove. Her response to the few one-night bookings she'd managed to get had already confirmed that. Granny Dugmore's notion of what was right and proper was an old problem. Sonia answered Alf. 'Yes, I think I'll give it a try.'

Granny Dugmore marched out into the back kitchen. 'Charlie, come and peel them potatoes,' she called to him.

Sonia rose. 'It's all right, Uncle Charlie. I'll do them.'

Granny Dugmore's voice came through the open door. '*Charlie* will do them.'

Charlie pulled a face and shook his head at Sonia. He mouthed silently, ''er's in a mood.' Alf giggled, and Charlie shook his fist at him. In spite of herself, Sonia was infected by Alf's giggle. She mouthed back: 'We know.' Out loud Charlie said he would do the potatoes, if they would get him some tobacco from the corner shop. They mouthed their reply in unison. 'Okay. Ta Ta For Now.' With their giggles threatening to burst out as laughter, they tiptoed out of the room.

They had a humbug-sucking competition on their way back from the shop. To see whose would last the longest.

'Let's have a look,' said Sonia. Alf gingerly showed his sweet on his tongue. 'You're cheating, I don't think you're sucking.'

'Yes I am. Let's see yours,' he replied.

'Oh, I give in. Mine's down to a bit of spit. You're the champ. Now finish it before we get in. Or I'll get a row for spoiling your appetite.'

Alf took out his humbug and admired it. 'Gran really will be in a mood if you get that job.'

'I know.'

'The stripes have gone now. Grandad Charlie says it's just the way she is. *He* doesn't mind you going off and singing and that.'

'How generous of him.'

'What do you mean?'

'I mean, it's not really any of their business, is it?' replied Sonia.

'I don't know, Mom, don't you like gran?'

Sonia sighed. She doubted whether she could explain. 'Yes, I like her. But you can like a person, and still not like some of the things they do and say. That's how I feel about gran. I think she probably feels the same about me.'

'I know what you mean,' said Alf.

'Do you?'

'It's like me and Grandad Charlie. I like him. I like him a lot. But I don't really like having to share a bedroom with him. He doesn't half snore.' Sonia smiled. 'And he smacks his lips. Like it was feeding time and you should put some food in.'

'It must run in the family. Gran's just the same when she's asleep.'

They stopped and laughed together. Sonia put her arm round Alf's shoulder, and they walked off, neatly in step. Automatically the rhythm of their stride began to resemble a stage routine. Soon they were varying their steps — big, small, forward, side — always together, keeping in time. 'Oh, we ain't got a barrel of . . . (Skip) . . . money. Maybe we're ragged and . . . (Knees bend) . . . funny. But we travel along . . . (Pause) . . . Singing a song . . . (Arms out) . . . Side by side.'

Alf spoke with a guttural accent. 'Hey, Hans — ve

34

had better break our step. Or ze pig-dog Englanders vill hear us.'

'Gut thinking, mein old pal.'

'Mom, Grandad Charlie said they ate people in the Boer War. The soldiers. *He* didn't, but he knew some who did. They had to because they were starving. Think of that.' He made a being sick noise.

Sonia grinned. 'When he told Dad that story, he said the soldiers *thought* they might have to. But then they were relieved.'

'When did he tell Dad that?'

'When he was about your age.'

'Did Dad believe him?'

'I think so.'

Alf spoke with a knowing voice. 'They would have been crazed by the sun's relentless rays.'

'What?'

'It was in a story I read about the desert. In Africa. The Boer War was in Africa.'

'Well, if I know Grandad Charlie, he would have been sitting under a nice shady tree,' she told him. 'Puffing his pipe and making up stories about how hard it was.'

'He got a medal,' Alf said. 'He showed me.'

'Everybody who came back got one,' replied Sonia.

Alf paused. 'That's not what he told me. He said he got it for being brave.'

'He's been pulling your leg. He used to do the same to Dad.' She ruffled his hair. 'So you see, you're not the only one who's been taken in.'

'You mean he's been lying?'

'Oh it's not like that. People like making up stories, and others like listening to them. Especially children.'

'Only when they're true.'

'Don't be daft. *You* invent things. Why shouldn't other people?'

Alf disagreed. 'Not if they're grown up. It's all right

35

for me, because I'm not. That's the difference between being young, and being grown up.'

'Dad does.'

He shook his head. 'Dad's different.'

'How?'

'Because he is.'

'I know one thing,' Sonia continued. 'When your father gets out of the army, he'll have at least as many stories as Grandad Charlie.'

'No he won't.'

'Of course he will. You know dad.'

'He won't, because they won't send him anywhere decent. Where there's fighting and that.'

'I certainly hope they don't,' said Sonia.

'They won't. He's in the Pioneer Corps. They don't give them rifles, they just get shovels. You ask Uncle Bill. He told me.'

'I bet *he* was pulling your leg as well.'

'No, he wasn't,' declared Alf. 'It was before dad went in, if you want to know. He said most of the time all they do is dig latrines. That's what they call lavatories.'

'I know what they are,' retorted Sonia. 'Anyway, that's not what dad said in his letter.'

'He wouldn't, would he?'

'I prefer to believe your father.'

'How do you know he wasn't telling one of his stories?' he replied, thinking himself very clever.

'Look here, it's time you stopped getting at dad. He's been a good father to you. Just because he didn't want to go in the army doesn't alter that. Lots of men don't want to go. You talk about truth. I'll tell you the truth. Nobody wants to be a hero — they'd rather stay at home.' Alf listened sullenly as she went on. 'Your trouble is, you get all you know from comics and films. Well, real people aren't like that. And adults know that. *That's* the difference between being young and grown up.'

They had reached the house and it was now totally dark. There was no problem in achieving a good blackout in Smethwick. Like the other towns around Birmingham, it had suffered badly from air-raids. Many of the streets had bombsites, and everyone knew someone who had been bombed out.

'Alf, I want you to promise, before we go in,' Sonia continued. 'You *will* write to dad?' She waited for his reply. 'All right?'

'All right.'

'Good,' said Sonia. She didn't see him shaking his head because of the darkness.

Charlie undid the top button of his trousers and belched.

'*Manners*,' said Granny Dugmore.

'I could go a bit o' spotted dick.' He poured tea from his cup into his saucer.

'Our Charlie, you've only just had the best meal we've had since the war started.'

'I know. But just to finish it off.' He supped from his saucer.

'That was lovely, Gran,' said Sonia.

Her mother-in-law beamed. Like the rest of them, she was enjoying the rare pleasure of feeling well fed. 'Thanks to our Alf. Though how he did it, I'll never know.'

Alf smiled mysteriously. 'Tricks of the trade Gran.'

'He gets more like our Dave every day, Glad,' said Charlie.

'He does an' all,' she agreed.

'It's lucky I found me teeth, Alf. I love a bit o' liver.'

'Couldn't you have eaten it without them Grandad Charlie?' asked Alf.

'Id've been here till breakfast time, chobbling away, if I hadn't had them in. Mind you, they'm giving me gyp now.' He took his teeth out and rubbed his gums.

'Charlie!'

'I'm here, not next door Glad. There's no need to shout.'

'Put them away at once.'

Alf rose from his place and went to Charlie. 'Let's have a look at them.'

'You don't want to go looking at them Alf,' said his gran.

'He can have a look if he wants,' said Charlie. 'Tek yours out an' all. There's nothing wrong with teeth.'

Granny Dugmore spoke to Sonia. 'He's that crude sometimes.'

'They're in two parts,' said Alf. 'They aren't joined together.'

Sonia interrupted. 'They're only like that in comics.'

'You couldn't swallow if they was,' said Charlie.

'I never thought about that,' replied Alf.

Sonia spoke to Alf. 'Give gran a humbug.'

Granny Dugmore waved the bag away. 'No, it's all right Sonia. It's not right, me using up the boy's points.'

'Have a chew o' tobacco then,' said Charlie, who was about to fill his pipe. He gave Alf a wink.

'*Can* you chew it Grandad Charlie? It smells rotten.'

'Not 'alf, you can. Puts hairs on your chest, a bit o' bacca.'

'Don't listen to him Alf,' warned his gran. 'He used to go on like that to your dad and Uncle Bill. He encouraged your dad to chew some tobacco once.'

'No I never. He took it himself.'

'Yes you did.'

'What happened?' Alf asked his gran.

'It was awful. Your dad was sick all over the settee, and Uncle Bill gave himself the bellyache laughing at him. They both got a leathering for that. And so should somebody else an' all,' she added with meaning.

Charlie leaned forward thoughtfully. 'The trouble was, Alf, your dad was the oldest, and he always had to show off to our Bill. Course Bill thought Dave was the cock o' the walk. So your dad *had* to be a bit of a daredevil, if you see what I mean.'

'When you put him up to it,' sniffed Granny Dugmore.

'D'you know what he did once, your dad? I'll tell you. You know the knobs on the front doors? Well, he went up and down the street, and he tied each pair together. You know how they'm side by side? Then he went and knocked on all the doors.'

Alf and Sonia laughed, and even Granny Dugmore smiled, as she tut-tutted at the memory.

'There wasn't half a carry-on. They got the policeman. Mind you, it didn't take him long to find who done it. You see, Dave hadn't thought to tie up his own front door. That did it. Our Bill piddled his britches when the copper come looking for Dave.'

'*Language* Charlie,' said Granny Dugmore.

'Did they take him to the police station?' asked Alf.

'No, the policeman just made him go to every house and say he was sorry. Most of them thought it was a good laugh. He did a little turn at some of the houses, and collected a couple o' bob in tips.'

'Did he Gran?'

'He did an' all,' she confirmed. 'I dunno how I managed sometimes. With the two of them, and me by meself.'

Charlie lit his pipe. 'They was good boys to you Glad.'

She sighed. 'I just hope to God they'm spared.' She took hold of Alf's hand. 'You see and remember to say your prayers for your dad and Uncle Bill.' He nodded. 'That's a good boy. Here. I'll show you something now.' She took an old Kodak envelope from behind

39

the clock on the mantelpiece. 'Here we are, some snaps of your dad and Uncle Bill.' She took the photographs out with great care. 'That's them when they was in the choir. There they are, in their cassocks and surplices. Look like little angels, don't they? If you knew the trouble I had getting them dressed up to have their snap took. Your dad said he only put it on for Sundays, weddings and funerals. Anything else would cost me extra. The cheeky varmint.'

Charlie chuckled. 'Dave always had a smashing voice. Not like poor old Bill. They had to throw him out of the choir. He put the others off.'

Sonia joined Alf at the table and looked at the photos with him. He took one out of a boy dressed in an army uniform. He was wearing a large walrus moustache.

'That was your dad,' said Granny Dugmore. 'Doing a turn. In the last war. Always up to something, he was. He's pretending to be "Old Bill". He used to be in all the cartoons in the papers.'

The next snap showed Dave on an improvised stage entertaining troops. 'How old was he there?' asked Sonia.

'About twelve or thirteen. Them soldiers were waiting to go to France. To the trenches. When our Dave sang "Keep The Home Fires Burning" they cried like babies.'

'It was our Bill's job to go round with the hat and collect the money,' said Charlie. 'Dave always made sure Bill looked dead poor, holes in his jersey and that. He said it helped their takings. Talk about a showman!'

Alf found himself feeling envious of this boy in the photographs. Whatever attitude he was caught in by the camera, he looked confident. Enjoying showing off his skill. 'Couldn't we do that Mom? Entertain the troops?'

'It's not the same now as it was in the last war.' It

was clear from Sonia's tone of voice she didn't want Alf to pursue the subject.

'They still need entertainers, Sonia,' said Charlie. 'To do shows for the boys.'

'See Mom, we could.'

'I don't think so,' she replied.

Charlie nodded at Alf. 'He's a chip of the old block Glad.'

'I bet we could,' Alf went on. 'And it would be easier than the halls.'

'No it wouldn't,' declared his mother.

'They wouldn't be expecting Dad in the act. That's why we lost all the bookings.' The look on his mother's face should have warned Alf to stop. But he was caught up with the idea and pushed on. 'Anyway, you said we couldn't stay at gran's for long.'

Granny Dugmore sat up. 'Whatever put that idea in your head Sonia?'

Sonia could have kicked Alf. She saw that he'd realised his mistake. However, it would have helped if he hadn't clapped his hand over his mouth. She spoke to her mother-in-law. 'We can't, can we, Gran? It's not fair on you. You've been smashing. You and Uncle Charlie making room for us. Having to share your bedrooms. I mean, there isn't enough room, is there?'

'That don't enter into it,' said Granny Dugmore brusquely. 'You'm our family.'

'I know Gran, and don't think I'm not grateful,' Sonia told her.

Charlie spoke. 'You'm not putting nobody out.'

'You've both been very kind . . .' Sonia went on.

'We've done our best, but it seems it's not been good enough for some people,' said Granny Dugmore, now sitting bolt upright in her chair.

Her self-righteous remark and sudden change made Sonia despair, as she recognised the beginning of yet another of her 'moods'. Having been at the receiving end of most of her mother-in-law's recent moods, Sonia knew the break had to come sooner rather than later. She attempted to reason with her.

'If I get the King's Highway job, I'll be coming in late at night, disturbing you. It's not fair. We've really got to move.'

'And what about Alf?' Granny Dugmore demanded. 'Who's going to look after him, with you gadding around in public houses?'

Sonia ignored the tone of what she said. 'I am quite capable of looking after my own son, thank you very much.'

'That's news to me,' replied Granny Dugmore. 'I know your sort — only time for number one. He'll end up hanging around outside the pub, waiting for you to finish. Like a slum kid.'

'Hold on Glad . . .' Charlie attempted to pacify his sister. 'Sonia's been a good mother to our Alf.'

'You won't change her mind, Uncle Charlie,' said Sonia. 'She's never approved of me performing. Even when I was with Dave on the halls. Oh, it's all right for a *man*. They can be on the stage, or in and out of pubs till they're blue in the face. But not a woman. It's common.'

'I'm not going to argue,' said Granny Dugmore. 'But I know what I think. And I know what other people think as well.'

'Oh yes. Don't let's forget the neighbours.'

Charlie tried again. 'I know, let's have another cup of tea. Alf, why don't you go and put the kettle on.'

'Be quiet Charlie,' said his sister. 'You stay where you are Alf. It's high time you saw what your mother is like.'

Sonia was shocked. 'What do you mean — see what I'm like? What are you getting at?'

'As if you didn't know,' sneered Granny Dugmore. 'Sitting there all tarted up in your make-up and silk stockings. And you call yourself a mother.'

Sonia fixed her mother-in-law with a look. 'So now we know where we stand. Well, I suppose I should be glad you've said it at last.'

There was a heavy silence. The two women seemed unsure how to proceed now that they had finally challenged each other. Charlie was sure Sonia didn't stand much of a chance. Nobody got the better of his sister. When they had been children together his nickname for her had been Gladys the Cow. He felt like using it to her now. But he knew he wouldn't. He couldn't risk losing his billet — not even for Sonia and Alf. He started to tidy up the photographs on the table. His sister stopped him and then spoke to Alf.

'Would you like some of these snaps of your dad, Alf? You *should* have some photos of your dad after all.'

Alf looked at his mother. She nodded and turned away from them towards the fire.

Granny Dugmore spoke to Alf as she went through the photographs. 'You have the ones you like. Now you're going to be took away from us, you should have some pictures of your dad and his family.' She took some more photographs out of the envelope. 'These are when your dad was older. Here he is in a concert party at Rhyl. And this is him in panto.' She held up the snap. 'Where was that, Charlie?'

'I dunno,' said Charlie uneasily.

Granny Dugmore went on. 'That was before he got married. We used to love going to see him, didn't we Charlie? We was always a close family. You ask your Uncle Bill. We'd go off and see him, whatever show he was in. He was a good lad. Always sent us tickets.'

Sonia turned from the fire and spoke to Alf. 'But then, your dad met this flighty bit of stuff called Sonia. Common as muck, she was. Dancing and showing her legs. And she led him astray. Do you remember Charlie? Didn't our Dave stop going to Sunday School just after he met her?'

Charlie couldn't handle Sonia's sarcasm, or his sister's insinuations. 'Look, both of you,' he appealed. 'Going on like this won't do no good.'

But Sonia went on regardless. 'The fact that their double act improved Dave's bookings didn't mean anything.' She imitated her mother-in-law's whining Black Country voice. '*Her dragged him down.* They got on the halls — made more money. But that made no difference. *Her was bad for our Dave her was.*'

'You think you'm very clever, don't you?' said Granny Dugmore.

'Say it!' retorted Sonia. 'I took your favourite son away from you.'

'At least I brought him up proper.'

'Not proper enough, it seems,' Sonia told her. 'He fell for me.'

'He was too good-natured — that was always his trouble,' said Granny Dugmore. 'That's how you managed to get your claws into him. You took advantage of his good nature.'

Sonia addressed Alf. 'There you are. That's what your grandmother thinks of your mother.'

'Leave Alf out of it.'

'You're the one who wanted him to see what I'm like, remember.'

'Take no notice of her Alf,' said Granny Dugmore.

'Don't you tell my son not to listen to his mother,' retorted Sonia.

Her mother-in-law banged her hand on the table. 'That's what *you* did to *my* son,'

'Rubbish. That's what you made yourself believe. Because you didn't want to lose him.'

Granny Dugmore turned angrily to Charlie. 'Her's wicked. Wicked. Did you hear what she said?'

Charlie shook his head sadly. 'I don't think much o' neither on you. Carrying on like this in front of the lad. Come on Alf, give us an 'and to do the crocks.'

Alf was halted by his gran. She took hold of his

shoulder and held him firm. 'Don't you forget what your mother's said here tonight. Just let it sink in. And when her lets you down, just you remember, you can always come back here to your gran.' She gave Sonia a vindictive look and let Alf go.

Alf went to his mother's side. 'You've got it wrong, Gran. It's not my mom. It's my dad who let me down,' he told her.

4

4917238 Dugmore D Pte
B Coy 2Bn Pioneer Corps
Colchester
28 Nov 1943

Dear Alf,

How are you?

Now mom's gone off, she's not been writing as much. Lucky her, back in the business, and me stuck here. I'd give my right arm to get into ENSA. How did she manage it? I've tried. I told the CO I'd be much better entertaining the troops in ENSA than trying to be a soldier. But it didn't do any good. I've done the odd turn for the boys here — but it ain't exactly show business. Mind you, it's helped a bit. Now they've seen I can do something, they don't think I'm such a drip any more! We've got a bloke here who plays the spoons. Just an amateur, but he's good. He's teaching me. I'll show you one day.

I often think about you and mom. I really do miss you. That's the worst bit about being away. The barracks and food could be worse. Fact is, they're better than some of the digs we stayed in. And the Sergeant-Major is an angel compared to some of those landladies! By the way, I heard from Uncle Bill. I can't tell you where he is, just that he's overseas. Anyway, poor old Bill's in the thick of it. But he sounds happy enough. Got no choice I suppose.

Mom told me Grandad Charlie's been telling you about the Boer War. Between you and me, when he used to go on about it to me, I used to call it the BORE WAR. (Big gag!)

I wasn't surprised you moved from gran's. She and mom never did get on. You'll like living with Dot and Amy. They're a right couple of cards. We used to have some good times together. Are they still working on their act? You should be able to give them a few tips — as an old pro!

Well, I'd better finish this off now and go and win the war, or have my tea. Drop me a line. I know your education has been mucked about a bit. But I seem to remember that you can write!!!

Lots of love,
Dad.

Alf was lying on his bed. He tucked his dad's letter under the mattress, which was stacked on top of nine other mattresses. He lay back and looked at the pictures he'd pasted on the ceiling. Because of the height of his bed, these were only a few feet above him. Errol Flynn grinned at him. Alf felt his upper lip and wondered if he would ever be able to grow a moustache. Flynn's moustache and flashing teeth were as important as his skill as a fighter in his screen battles. On the other hand, whiskers were stupid. You didn't need them. Unless you were Desperate Dan and used them to strike matches. But that didn't really work. Alf had tried it on Grandad Charlie's stubble when he was having a nap.

There was a programme from Liverpool Empire showing *Sonia, Dave and Sonny* half way up the bill. Aston Villa were there; as were the Warwickshire County cricket team. A Spitfire chased a Messerschmidt. And a Crusader tank stood bleakly in the desert. This was in his picture collection because Grandad Charlie worked in the factory where they

47

were made. A piece of information that Alf *shouldn't* have known, but *did*. Thanks to Grandad Charlie asking if he could keep a secret. Alf had sworn to himself never to pass this on to the Germans, no matter what they did to him.

He climbed down the ladder he'd made for getting in and out of bed. His room was the remains of what had been the store behind a furniture shop. The shop had been almost completely destroyed in the blast from a bomb that had fallen in the street outside. A wooden partition had been put up to separate the damaged area from the storeroom. Officially the storeroom was locked up, the owner being away in the forces. Alf had moved in thanks to Dot and Amy, who had said they would look after the store. They had a small flat at the back of the building.

Alf opened one of the seven wardrobes and took out some of the firewood he kept stored there. He'd given each wardrobe, chest of drawers and dressing-table its own special use. He took newspapers from one drawer and matches from another, and lit his fire. When it was going nicely, he went into the flat and did the same for Dot and Amy, who would soon be home from work.

Back in his own room he used his dirty hands to darken his face. He checked the result in several dressing-table mirrors. Not much like a commando. He added a little soot from around the fireplace. He'd only just heard about these specially selected soldiers. They were super tough and gave the impression that they could walk through walls without flinching. To copy the knitted woollen hat they wore, he used one of Dot's long winter socks. He knew they sometimes used daggers, preferring to inflict death by stealth. A piece of firewood would do for that. He put it in his mouth and glowered at the numerous mirrors. A small platoon of mucky-faced boys glowered back at him. Each one of them aware of what an unpleasant taste firewood has.

Outside it was dusk and the bombsite became Alf's battlefield. As Sergeant Mike Dugmore he was the commander of a small section of devil-may-care toughguys, renowned throughout the Allied armies. This was much more satisfying than being a general. *They* had to spend too much time bossing people about and never getting into the thick of things. The granite-jawed sergeant, on the other hand, was always in with the action. He briefed his dedicated band of men. (Each one hand-picked, and permitted to call him Mike when the going got rough.) The objective tonight was to scale the cliffs and *eliminate* an enemy machine-gun post. They were going to cook Jerry's goose for him. There were murmurs of approval from the men. Mike grinned. The patrol set off.

The hundred-foot-high cliffs proved no problem. The battle-hardened veterans took them in their stride. But the machine-gun post was not so easy. Assessing the situation, Mike knew it was impossible for the whole section to approach it unobserved. It would have been suicide. But one man might just make it . . . One man who knew exactly what was at stake. Who had courage and, most important of all — guts. A man who'd teach those Germans a lesson they'd never forget. He told his men there was only one thing for it. He would go in alone. Fingering the stubble on his chin, he listened grimly to their gasps of admiration. Some of them managed to choke out a few words, begging him not to go. He grinned, and shook his head. This was something he'd got to do alone. He clasped his dagger between his teeth and set off. Within a few moment he froze . . . He'd been biting so hard his dagger had split. He threw it away and spat out a few splinters. Undeterred, he knew he would have to go in and finish them off with his bare hands. He thought of his men, each willing him to succeed. Again he flashed the grin they had come to know and love. He would not let them down. It's chaps like that who make it all worthwhile . . .

'GOTCHA!'

Alf felt himself being lifted and frogmarched off the bombsite and up the entry beside the ruined furniture shop. Dot and Amy were on either side of him and one of them was tickling him. He begged for mercy. They dumped him on the settee in the flat.

'The nerve. That's my sock,' said Dot. 'And look at your face.'

'That's how commandos camouflage themselves.'

'Looks more like you stuck your head up the chimney,' said Amy. 'Put the kettle on somebody. This war effort will be the death of me.' Amy worked as a nurse at Nettlefold's factory. Her friend Dot was the assistant manageress in the works canteen. 'I had a queue wanting attention all day. And what about you Dot?'

'Well, strange as it may seem, everybody wanted feeding. Same as usual.'

'There's no accounting for people,' said Amy.

'However . . .' Dot picked up her shopping bag. 'A roll of drums and fanfare if you please.' The other two obliged, as she did a magic pass over the bag and pulled out an apple tart. 'How about that?'

'Quick, get a knife Alf,' said Amy.

'Hold on, it's for our pudding,' Dot told her.

'Well, let's have our pudding *first,* for a change.'

'Give this woman a prize,' replied Dot. '*Anybody* can have their pudding second. It takes real genius to hit on the idea of having it first. Taking the knife from my young assistant here, I will do the honours.'

'What's your dad say in his letter?' asked Amy, when they were seated round the fire, tucking into the tart. Alf told them.

'Jammy old Dave,' said Dot, who was Dave's cousin. 'It didn't take him long to work a cushy number.'

'Not half,' agreed Amy. 'And I bet poor Bill's copping it. Same as usual. He never had any luck.'

'What do you mean?' asked Alf.

'Your dad's always been one up on your Uncle Bill.'

'But Uncle Bill's a corporal now.'

Dot was not impressed. 'A couple of stripes aren't worth getting yourself stuck up the sharp end. With all them Germans taking pot-shots at you. No fear. Your dad's far better off.'

'Somebody's got to do the fighting,' said Alf.

Dot licked the crumbs of pastry from her fingers. 'That's right, somebody else — not me, as the man said.'

'I'd fight,' said Alf.

'You'll learn,' Dot told him.

'I'd blast the Germans to smithereens,' he replied, throwing an imaginary grenade and making the sound of the explosion.

Dot got up. 'I'll drop a note to Mr Churchill about you. Now, I'm off to fry up our second course. After that we'll have a go at "Cinderella",' she added on her way to the kitchen.

An area of Alf's room was kept clear of furniture. Not an easy task. It meant that some of the stacks of chairs and other units were piled dangerously high. The tiny space was known grandly as 'the stage'. And it was here that Dot and Amy rehearsed their double act. At present they only performed in the works canteen, but one day they hoped to be good enough to turn pro and go on the halls.

'The girls', as they liked to be known, had involved Alf as soon as he'd moved in and currently they were rehearsing a slapstick version of 'Cinderella' for three people. Privately Alf had his doubts about whether the audience would find it funny. But he held his tongue. Dot and Amy had been very kind to him and he didn't want to hurt them.

Alf opened one of the wardrobes labelled PANTO PROPS and took out a ragged dress adorned with brightly coloured patches. He groaned, but put it on nevertheless. Next he lifted a wig of long golden hair from the wardrobe and placed it on his head. He decided to leave his face dirty, concluding that Cinders would have had a dirty face anyway. Then he sat down moodily and waited for the girls, who were putting on their costumes in the flat.

He hadn't wanted to act a girl, but Dot and Amy had argued that they were too big, and he couldn't very well be an Ugly Sister or the Prince. So reluctantly he'd had to put up with it. The thing that annoyed him about Cinders was that she was so *stupid*. A boy wouldn't have put up with half of what she suffered — *he* certainly wouldn't. He would have told the Ugly Sisters what he thought of them and run away.

There was a knock at the door and Alf switched off the light. This was necessary because of the blackout, the bomb-damaged entry being open to the sky. Dot and Amy clattered in, bumping into everything in their crinolines and as soon as the light was on again they started rehearsing.

They had based the Ugly Sisters on the two enemy dictators, Hitler and Mussolini — convinced the audience would find this a big joke. Secretly Alf had his doubts about this, believing the idea had been 'done to death', as they said on the halls. But he kept these thoughts to himself and threw himself into his performance. He enjoyed striding about the stage sobbing his heart out and telling the audience he couldn't go to the ball. After this he blew his nose loudly on a much-patched hankie and flung himself down in front of an imaginary fireplace.

'Pull your skirt down, I can see your trousers,' hissed Amy.

Dot entered wearing a small Hitler moustache and goose-stepped across to Cinders.

'Vot you doink, makink this horrible noise?' she bawled. 'Ven you should my hair for the ball be preparing.'

Alf clasped his hands together and grovelled on his knees. 'Please let me go to the ball with you. Please, oh please, kind Hitleria.'

'Vot a cheek this girl has,' declared Dot Hitleria.

Alf sobbed. 'I'll clean the house, wash the black-out curtains, and decorate the air-raid shelter,' he told her.

'Dumpkopf!' shrieked Dot. 'Kitchen maids to the ball do not go. It is only for posh pretty people, like me and my sister Musso.'

'She stole my clothing coupons to make her dress,' said Alf.

Hitleria snorted. 'A rag-bag like you is not coupons needing.'

'How can you be so cruel?' asked Cinders sadly.

'Very easily!' laughed Hitleria. 'Ve are very good at being bad!'

Amy clonked on wearing army boots under her crinoline. She kicked Cinders out of the way and kissed her sister at least ten times on each cheek. Hitleria borrowed Cinders' hankie and wiped her face.

'Musso, my favourite sister!' twittered Hitleria.

Musso thrust out her booted foot at Cinders. 'What's a-going on here? I looka under the bed for-a my party shoes. And whata do I see? There they are gone! All I gotta left are my slippers. I can'ta go dancing in these!' she said, stamping her feet in fury.

Cinders answered her. 'Don't you remember, Musso? When I told Hitleria that the dustbin was full up she said I could use your party shoes instead.'

Musso glared at Hitleria. 'You German sausage!' she cried.

'You Italian salami!' replied her sister.

The two of them squared up to each other like a couple of heavyweight boxers and Alf, as Cinders, was supposed to act like a referee at a boxing match. The idea was that they had a comic fight and ended up with them both getting knocked out at the same time. As a gag it wasn't bad, but the thing that worried Alf was that Dot and Amy never seemed to do the same thing twice. They kept inventing new bits at each rehearsal and then forgetting them.

'Seconds out — round one!' said Alf, giving a ting on a little bell.

The sisters eyed each other and shuffled round snorting.

'Break!' shouted Alf.

'What do you mean — break?' asked Amy. 'We haven't even touched each other yet.'

'I know. That's why I thought it would be funny,' said Alf.

'*We're* supposed to be the funny ones,' said Dot.

The fight started again with Hitleria waving her arms like a windmill, and Musso dodging this way and that to avoid her. Musso's intention was to use her big boots to some effect and kick Hitleria on the backside. The pace hotted up and they started to rush across the stage, just missing each other in the middle. The last time they had rehearsed the fight they had decided that it would be funny if Alf got caught up in this, so he positioned himself centre stage. However, on their next charge at each other, it appeared that Dot and Amy had forgotten what they had done before. Instead of twirling Cinders round, Hitleria and Musso went all out for their knockout blows.

'Donner und Blitzen!' yelled Dot as she charged.

'Spaghetti and chips!' screamed Amy.

And they met in the middle, crushing Alf like the buffers between two tank engines.

When they parted Alf slumped to the floor wondering if he would ever be able to breathe again.

'What were you doing there?' Dot asked him.

Unable to speak for the moment and fed up with the rehearsal, Alf considered doing his fainting routine. But he decided against it — Amy was a nurse and she would have found him out. Instead he staggered to his feet and indicated in mime that he would go and make a cup of tea.

Putting the kettle on in the flat, he noticed Dot's sock and took off his wig. Pulling the sock on his head he immediately became Sergeant Mike again. Grinning at himself in the mirror, he felt the bristles on his chin and explained to his men the reason for his disguise. He'd fool the German patrol into thinking he was a French waitress and when they came into the café, he would blast them all to smithereens. No . . . he wouldn't need any men to help him. He was going to do this one on his own. It'd be a piece of cake . . .

Going to one school was a big change for Alf. When he'd been on the halls he lost count of how many schools he had attended, since he went to a different one each week. He'd hated Monday mornings — never knowing what sort of school he would end up in. On one marvellous occasion the school he was due to go to had been damaged in an air-raid and, like the rest of the children, he'd had an extra week's holiday. It was the one decent thing that had happened to him since the war began. Unfortunately he'd never had such luck again and he'd dreaded the awful moment when some head teacher opened the strange classroom door and pushed him inside. Every eye in the room fixed on him . . . sizing him up. The smirks and giggles when his name was announced to the teacher. Then finding himself sharing a desk with someone he didn't know. And the first playtime . . . Would they leave him alone — or pick a fight?

He'd been glad to settle into the security of Bearwood Road Junior School, with its white-tiled hall and brown-varnished classrooms, each with a map of the British Empire and sad-looking nature tables. Alf enjoyed being an ordinary pupil, rather than a temporary oddity. It was a new experience for him to be accepted as one of the boys, and before long he found himself looked upon as a natural leader. This was due mainly to the fact that he could make them laugh, rather than as his skill as a fighter. Because of his experience on the stage, he had cocky confidence and a way with words that left his classmates gawping at his skill.

On the last day before they broke up for the Christmas holidays there was to be a service after morning playtime and a school party in the afternoon. After she had called the register, Alf's teacher, Mrs Kenrick, set her class the task of silent reading so that they would not get too excited. But the silence was soon broken by a rap on the door and the school nurse walked into the room. She whispered to Mrs Kenrick, who nodded and addressed one of the girls in the class.

'Audrey Sutton — you're to go along with the nurse.'

There was a babble of interest from the class when they heard this. The nurse was only slightly less menacing than the dentist and they were desperate to know what terrible fate awaited Audrey.

'Audrey — did you hear what I said?' asked Mrs Kenrick.

The class craned their heads to see Audrey, who was still sitting at her desk. Unlike the rest, who shared desks in pairs, she sat by herself.

'Smelly Wellies,' said Alf behind his hand and the group around him sniggered. It was their nickname for Audrey, who came from a slum family and always wore a pair of old wellies, whatever the weather.

'That will do,' said Mrs Kenrick to the class, as she went down the aisle between the desks. 'Come along. The nurse is waiting,' she told Audrey sharply.

The girl shook her head and wouldn't move.

'Audrey, if I have to tell you again . . .'

The nurse came down the aisle, interrupting Mrs Kenrick. 'Come on my girl!' she said, taking Audrey's arm and pulling her to her feet.

'No!' Audrey screamed.

By now the children on the other side of the room were standing up to get a better view of the scene.

'Don't be such a silly girl,' said Mrs Kenrick. 'The nurse only wants to see you for a moment.'

'Her wants to cut my hair off!' Audrey shouted in reply.

'That's nonsense . . .'

'*Will you come along* . . .' The nurse tugged her up the aisle, with Audrey trying to pull and kick herself free. 'Mrs Kenrick, I'm going to report this child to the Head!' puffed the nurse, struggling with the hysterical girl.

The class listened in morbid fascination as the screaming Audrey was hauled out of the classroom and taken across the hall to the medical inspection room. Some of them held their noses, while others made a show of scratching their hair, being sure that Audrey had been taken away because she had head lice — or nits, as they were known.

'*That will do*,' commanded Mrs Kenrick. 'If I do not have absolute silence until playtime, there will be *no* playtime and *no* milk.'

Her threat worked. Which meant that by the time the children got into the playground, they charged around working off their pent-up energy and excitement. Doubtless with Audrey in mind, the girls started a game of Stinky-tick — a kind of tag in which you had to hold your nose if you were caught. As usual the boys preferred something rougher and paired off into piggyback couples to play tanks and batter each other into the ground.

By the time Audrey came out into the playground it

was alive with activity and she stayed by herself near the door. She made no move to join in the girls' game and nobody asked her to take part. She had stopped crying, but her face was tear-stained and there were smudges of white powder on her cheeks and forehead. These were the result of the 'dusting' the nurse had given her hair, which now appeared grey in places from the powder that had been rubbed into her scalp. Automatically her hand went to her mouth and she nibbled at her nails, only stopping now and again to sniff.

As they became aware of Audrey, the girls stopped playing and stared at her, whispering and giggling amongst themselves. They knew better than to say anything out loud and risk getting into a fight with Audrey.

Most of the tanks had been knocked over and the boys were in a noisy heap on the ground. As they struggled to their feet there was a loud burst of laughter, and some of the boys pointed at Audrey in their mirth.

'Go on — sing it again Alf!' shouted one of them.

'Yeah — go on Alf!' chorused the others.

The boys clustered in a group around Alf, urging him on, and he began the song he'd just made up, sung to the tune of the popular ditty 'The Quartermaster's Stores'.

> There were nits, nits,
> Having blooming fits,
> In Audrey's hair, in Audrey's hair.
> There were nits, nits,
> Having blooming fits,
> In Aud-rey Sutt-on's hair!

With a bellow of laughter the boys joined in the chorus.

'Do another one Alf — go on!'

Relishing being the centre of attention and admired by his pals, Alf came up with an even better verse.

There were nits, nits,
Doing the splits . . .

This time the girls laughed out loud as well as the boys, and joined them in singing the second verse. Then the bell went and they had to stop and get into their class lines.

As the boys were thumping his back and congratulating him, Alf caught a glimpse of Audrey. She returned his look with a stare that felt as if she was trying to see inside him.

A model of the nativity scene had been set up in the school hall and Alf's attention was drawn to it during the Christmas service. He thought a stable would be a good place to sleep — hay smelt nice and kept you warm. And being near a desert, Bethlehem wouldn't have been too cold anyway, unlike Smethwick in December. Three wooden dolls represented the Wise Men, but they didn't have any gifts. When the vicar got to that bit of the story, Alf wondered what on earth frankincense and myrrh looked like. And what good would they be to a baby? He could understand the gift of gold. Mary would be able to use that to buy things for Jesus, or it would have come in useful if Joseph had wanted to get another donkey.

They sang 'Away In A Manger' and you could tell it was everyone's favourite carol from the way it echoed around the hall. Alf certainly liked it. The tune was good and there weren't any difficult words, like you got in a lot of hymns. When it ended the vicar smiled at the children and asked them to remain standing. And then his face became serious, and he began speaking about the war. Alf knew what was coming and he tried not to listen, but he heard every word, as though the vicar was speaking to him personally. At this time of rejoicing, we must not forget those brave men and women in the armed services, who were at that very moment fighting to defend our beloved country. He used words like courage, duty, and sacrifice, to emphasise the debt everyone owed them.

Alf had lied to his school friends about his father. As he saw it, he'd had no choice. How could he admit Dave didn't want to fight, knowing they had fathers and relatives in the forces overseas? He'd kept quiet about his dad being dumped in the Pioneer Corps and told them he was certain Dave was doing hush-hush work testing secret weapons. And they'd believed him. With his talent for making up stories it had been easy to fool them.

'Let us pray . . .' The vicar's voice took on the special tone he kept for prayer and the children bowed their heads.

The vicar asked God to remember their loved ones and keep them safe. With his eyes closed and his hands clasped in front of him, Alf saw his father clearly in his mind's eye. As ever, it was Dave with a smile on his face, as though he'd just told one of his jokes. Alf couldn't remember him any other way and he wanted to yell at Dave that there were more important things in life than telling gags. You couldn't laugh off being a coward — not if you were a proper man.

He peeped along the row as the vicar's prayer went on. Some of the class with parents in the services were crying. Alf looked away from them guiltily and squeezed his eyes shut. The nice warm feeling he'd had singing the carol might never have happened.

'We will conclude our service with a hymn. A hymn that has always given comfort in troubled times. It reminds us that God is on our side and will help us to fight the good fight. "O God our help in ages past, Our hope for years to come".'

The piano hammered out the opening chord and after a tentative beginning, the singing swelled in volume and filled the hall with triumphant sound.

Alf's lips hardly moved and the hymn's stirring words meant nothing to him. The realisation had come to him that he could not now turn to God for help. Seeing his friends' tears had convinced him. God would help *them,* he was sure of it. But He was unlikely to do much to help a liar. He might as well forget praying for a miracle to change everything.

The party in the afternoon did not cheer him up. He played the games and danced the Hokey Cokey, but his mood persisted and he was glad when it was hometime and they were dismissed. He'd often been told by his mother not to 'feel sorry for himself' — as though it was a crime to be unhappy. But that was exactly what he felt, as he hung behind after the others had rushed out through the school gates. The misery, that had begun with the Christmas service, welled up inside him and he hid himself behind the empty bike shed and burst into tears.

When he eventually dried his eyes and blew his nose, he realised that someone had seen him. It was Audrey. She had been watching him from across the playground. Filled with anger he ran after her, determined to make her pay — not only for seeing him crying, but everything else as well. He chased along eagerly, thankful to have a way of working off his frustration on somebody else. But he was denied that pleasure. Audrey easily gave him the slip in the crowds doing their Christmas shopping in Bearwood Road.

5

Alf was digging on the bombsite for Christmas presents. There must have been a lot of ornaments on display in the furniture shop before it was destroyed. Most of the china ones had been broken. But with luck you could come up with something that was still whole, or only slightly damaged. There were also brass and copper pieces, and some of these had survived very well. He'd just found a miniature Dutch clog and this gave him hope. He thought the idea of getting his presents like this was brilliant. It wouldn't cost a penny, and they would be things he wouldn't normally be able to afford. However, the work was not easy. The rubble was difficult to shift.

He got up and stretched his aching legs. He decided to try another part of the site. His attention was caught by what appeared to be an old box, or chest. Immediately thoughts of buried treasure flashed across his mind and he hurriedly started to dig out the box.

As more of it came into view, it really did begin to resemble a treasure chest. Alf felt a shiver of excitement. What if . . .? He pretended to dismiss the notion, telling himself that people didn't keep hidden treasure in furniture shops. You had to have a desert island, or a forest with a gnarled oak tree to bury treasure properly. Still . . . you never knew. 'There's a first time for everything.' He'd often heard Grandad Charlie say that. He paused in his digging and crossed all his fingers and thumbs. Pirates, he knew, went on about 'pieces of eight'. Eight what? Could you take a piece of eight into a shop in olden days? And what about if what you were buying cost less? What did you get for change? He remembered seeing Errol Flynn opening up a pirate treasure chest. It had been full of brightly coloured jewels. That would be awful. If Dot and Amy saw jewels they'd go off their heads and he wouldn't get a look in. Maybe he should cover the chest up again?

But his curiosity got the better of him and he carried on. Soon he was able to get his hands round the chest and work it free. It was about the size of a biscuit tin and quite heavy. He shook it and could tell there was something inside. He tried to open the lid, but it was locked. A bent key was sticking out of the lock, but it wouldn't turn all the way round and release the lid. The Lone Ranger would have shot the lock off with his Colt revolver. All Alf could do was kick it.

'What are you up to then?'

Alf turned, and there, halfway across the bombsite, was his Uncle Bill. He was in uniform and leaning on a walking stick. Alf forgot the box and ran to him over the rubble.

'Uncle Bill! What are you doing here?'

'Visiting you, kid,' Bill told him.

'You've got a walking stick,' said Alf.

'You should have seen me last week. I had crutches then.'

'Were you wounded?' asked Alf, his eyes wide.

'Yes. So they gave me a bit of leave,' replied Bill cheerfully.

Alf didn't know what to do to express his feelings. He couldn't kiss Uncle Bill. And shaking his hand would have been daft. His uncle was having the same problem. After a moment's hesitation he put his arm round Alf's shoulder and gave him an awkward hug. Alf risked clasping his uncle's other hand that was holding the walking stick. They broke apart and grinned at each other.

'What are you doing?' asked Bill.

'Digging for things. I've found a box, but I can't get it open.'

'Let's have a look.'

Alf brought the box to his uncle. He had to hold it up because Bill couldn't stoop down to it on the ground. Bill took out an amazing penknife that seemed to have six of everything and selected a screwdriver blade. He slotted it into the loop at the end of the key and turned. The extra leverage popped the lock open in a second. Alf opened the lid. He almost fainted when his eye caught a glimpse of gold.

'Just look at that,' said Bill. 'That's amazing. Beautiful.' The inside of the box was divided into sections, from which Bill took out a handful of brass nails and screws and upholstery pins. 'There's loads, look. And all different sizes.'

In spite of his disappointment, Alf was surprised at his uncle's reaction. 'I thought it might be buried treasure,' he said.

His uncle smiled. 'Tough luck. Though, mind you, in a way it *is*. You couldn't buy brass nails and screws for love nor money these days. Not since the war started. Be just about worth its weight in gold this lot.'

Alf brightened up. 'Could we sell it?'

'Leave it to me,' said Bill. 'I'll get you a few quid for it.' He put the nails and screws carefully back into their sections. 'It makes you think. We used to take stuff like this for granted before the war.'

In the flat Bill eased himself into an armchair. He couldn't bend his injured leg and it remained stuck out in front of him. Alf made them a cup of tea.

'Will you have to go back Uncle Bill?'

'Oh yes. They'll put me on light duties, I suppose.'

'So you won't have to do any more fighting?' asked Alf.

'I shouldn't think so.'

'Who did you enjoy fighting the most — the Italians or the Germans?'

'I didn't enjoy any of it,' Bill told him, shaking his head. 'It's more a matter of putting up with it. Still, I suppose you could say the Italians were the easiest. You could tell their heart wasn't in it. Poor devils. When they surrendered they were as happy as could be.'

'Even when you beat them?'

'They didn't care about that. They were just glad to be alive. They had smiles all over their faces most of the time. We liked them. They cheered us up no end.'

Alf poured out their tea and took a cup to his uncle. 'I saw Italian prisoners of war on the newsreel. There were thousands of them.'

Bill sipped his tea. 'Ah, that's better. Yes, that's right. I was a guard on a prisoner of war cage for a while. In North Africa. That was a a laugh. We used to give them our rifles to look after while we went for a swim.'

'The prisoners? Honest?'

'Sure.'

Alf shook his head. 'You're pulling my leg.'

'It's true. I'm not kidding.'

'And they didn't escape?'

'No fear. They knew which side their bread was buttered on.'

'Fancy not trying to escape,' said Alf.

'They just wanted the war to end. Where could they escape to — the Germans? They hate them as much as we do.'

'But they were on their side,' said Alf, confused.

'Their government was. I don't think the ordinary Italians wanted to fight at all,' Bill told him. 'I'll tell you one thing, I wouldn't mind living in Italy after the war.'

Alf found it hard to believe his ears. His uncle was having him on. Nobody could want to go and live *there*. Everybody knew the Italians were oily cowards.

'You're pulling my leg again,' said Alf.

'I'm not. Honest. It was great when we got to Italy. After North Africa. The sun, the wine. Think of it, you can just reach out and pick a bunch of grapes if you want. The blue sky. You know Alf, they have these little farms and grow their crops on terraces, as neat as ninepence. But it's the weather and the bright colours you notice most. I'll never settle here now I've seen that. Now I know there's something else, you won't catch me putting up with Brum.'

Alf launched a patriotic counter-attack. 'Is that where you got wounded — in *Italy*?' He was sure this cunning question would restore Bill's common sense.

'Yes.'

'What happened?'

Bill put down his cup and saucer. He didn't seem keen to answer and Alf wondered if he was having second thoughts about Italy. Bill rubbed his wounded leg, as though the memory of how it had happened made it painful. Alf remained silent.

Bill began to speak. 'We were supposed to capture this hill. The platoon. Our platoon commander had been killed. So the sergeant had taken over. Sergeant Bates, he was a mate of mine. I was in charge of one of the sections. Well, we seemed to be stuck and there wasn't much cover. And the Germans had a machine-gun up there. That was how Mr Willis, the officer, had copped it. So Batesy passes the word round to stay low. We'd have a crack at getting up when it got dark. We weren't too keen about that, I can tell you. Come dusk, Batesy decides to go up and have a bit of a look. To find the best route for us. It was fine. No shooting. Nothing. One of the lads said Jerry must be having his tea. Well, we waited and waited. In the end when he came back, he was dead chuffed. Said it was as safe as houses. Anyway, I was to take my section up the route he gave me. He was going across to Harry, the other corporal, to get him to follow on. And that was it. As he moved off across the hill, he trod on a mine. All I remember was a flash, I didn't even hear the explosion, and then waking up in the dressing station. At first I couldn't feel my leg and I was sure I'd lost it. But that was just the effect of the stuff the MO had given me. Then they told me. Batesy was killed. They never found his body.'

Bill nodded at his cup. 'Give us another, Alf.'

'Did you get your own back on those Germans with the machine-gun?' asked Alf.

'I reckon they'd done a bunk, even before we started up the hill,' said Bill. 'D'you know what the CO asked me to do? When he knew I was getting sent home. He wanted me to go and see Mrs Bates, Batesy's missus. He caught me on the hop, I can tell you. In the end I said I'd think about it. But I'm pretty sure he knew I wouldn't. I mean, what could I say to her? I'm no good at that kind of thing. In any case, she doesn't want to see me. I'd be sticking my nose in. She wouldn't want that, would she?'

Alf shook his head. *He* wouldn't have known what to say either. He remembered the mad landlady who'd lost her husband. Nobody could speak to *her*. Well, another woman might. It was the kind of thing they seemed to be able to do. Somehow they knew what to say. His mom was good at that sort of stuff. He was glad men could get out of it.

'Here's your tea uncle.'

'Ta, mate. You make a good cuppa. Dot and Amy have got you well trained.'

'Not 'alf!'

Bill laughed. 'So, after the war, you'll be able to

come to Italy for your holidays. Make a change from Rhyl!'

'I'll never go there. Or Germany, or Japan.'

'We'll see. That's been the one good thing the war's done for me,' said Bill. 'It's let me go abroad.'

'You wouldn't be able to go up the County Ground in Italy.'

His uncle gave another laugh. 'That's a thought. Still, you never know. Maybe I could teach the Eyeties to play cricket.'

Alf pulled a face. 'They'd be rotten. I bet they'd be scared of the hard ball.'

'And they don't drink tea. So I don't know what we'd do about the tea interval.'

'They'd have spaghetti and ice-cream!' Alf doubled up with mirth at his own joke.

'Hey, that'd be a good one for your dad to do,' said Bill. 'He'd be great at that. Taking the mickey out of the Italians playing cricket. You should suggest it to him. Up the Naples County Ground — knocking 'em for *sei*!'

'Is that six in Italian?' asked Alf.

'Yes. See — I speaka da lingo!'

'Say some more.'

'*Buon giorno*. Where isa da testa matcha?'

Alf threw a playful punch at his uncle. 'That's not Italian!'

'Bet you it is.'

'And I bet a million pounds it isn't!'

His uncle got him in an arm lock. 'It *is*. *Say* it . . . come on . . .'

'I give in — it is, it is! Let go!' Alf shouted out in mock pain.

But Bill didn't let him go. He slackened his hold slightly, but still held Alf firm. 'Now, something else. You've got to promise . . . and I'm not going to take no for an answer. I want you to promise to write to your dad.' Alf groaned. 'I couldn't believe it when

68

gran told me. Just think how your dad feels. A letter means a lot when you're fed up and far from home.'

'He's not fighting.'

'That doesn't make a blind bit of difference. Sixty per cent of the army's not fighting, dumbo. D'you think *their* families are not writing to them?' Alf didn't answer and Bill tightened his hold slightly. 'Well?'

'. . . no,' Alf mumbled.

'And I bet your mom's been on at you. You're letting her down as well. So, you've got to pull up your socks and write to him. Okay?' Alf nodded. 'Come on, say it.'

'All right.'

Bill let him go and smiled. '*Molte grazie.*'

The Christmas concert took place in the works canteen. It was timed so that when it ended, the night-shift would start work, and so loss of production would be kept down to a minimum. The stage was small, but serviceable. It had been built by volunteers and they had taken pride in doing a good job. The proscenium curtains were bright and cheerful and above them were painted the words 'Theatre Royal'. Unfortunately the theatrical atmosphere was not helped by the ever-present smell. The canteen was in use day and night, and hardly an hour passed when food was not being prepared, served, and cleared up. In one sense, the concert added to the prevailing odour, mixing in the exotic smells of greasepaint and powder with cabbage and peas. This was strongest in the area of the kitchen that was being used as a temporary dressing room. Here the performers got themselves ready to go on stage, side by side with the kitchen staff who were preparing dinner for the night-shift.

Alf and the girls were due to go on last. Or 'Top Of The Bill', as Dot and Amy insisted. They loved the hustle and bustle of getting ready and took ages. Or so it seemed to Alf.

He heard the audience applaud a fat man in an evening dress suit who had just sung 'Trees'. He sniggered to himself, remembering his dad's comment about it. He'd called it the dogs' theme song. Imagine writing a song about *trees*. If you could do that, you might as well write about trams, telegraph poles, air-raid shelters, bombs . . . The local comedian who was compering the show started telling Black Country stories. Alf didn't bother to listen. He was much more interested in the smell of frying sausages that drifted towards him. Like the kids in the Bisto advertisement, he traced it to its source. A woman in a white overall was unwrapping and frying more sausages than Alf had ever seen in his life.

'Hullo,' said Alf.

'Aren't you going to give us a curtsey then?' asked the woman with a laugh. Her face was red and damp strands of hair hung down from her cap.

'I'm really a boy.'

'I know. We've heard about you from Dot. Haven't we, Else?'

'Not 'alf,' said Else, who was putting cooked sausages onto plates.

''er said you bin on the halls with Tessie O'Shea and Arthur Askey and everybody.'

'Yes. That's right.' He felt flattered.

'Fancy, Else,' said Marge.

'Fancy,' said Else. 'Here, could you give us your whatsit? Your what-do-you-call-it? You know, on a bit of paper?'

''er means your autograph,' explained Marge.

Alf agreed. His first autograph! Else looked for something to write on.

'Here,' said Marge. She unwrapped the greaseproof paper from around some sausages and tore a piece off. She passed it to him with a pencil. Alf signed it with a flourish. 'Put "To Marjory and Elsie" on it,' she added.

Alf panicked. How did you spell Marjory? He played for time. 'I tell you what, I'll write it if you'll give me a sausage.'

'You can have as many as you like,' said Marge. 'But write it first, so's it don't get any more greasy.'

He scribbled 'To Margerey and Elsy'. However, he never knew if they were able to decipher it. Just as he was never to get a taste of their sausages. No sooner had he handed the paper back, than he heard his mother's name being spoken by the compere. It boomed through the loudspeakers at him. He ran through the kitchen as quickly as he could. When he got to the side of the stage the man was still speaking. ' . . . her ENSA tour. Sonia tells me she's performed in camps up and down the country. Entertaining our boys and those of our gallant allies. I might tell you, ladies and gentlemen, Sonia's only just arrived home for a few days' holiday. And she came here to *see* the show! However, after a little persuasion, she gamely volunteered to give us a number! Are you there, Sonia?' He peered into the audience. Through a crack in the curtain Alf saw his mom stand up. She was beside Uncle Bill. Stepping over Bill's stiff leg, she made her way to the stage. The compere led the audience. 'Let's give a big hand for Sonia Dugmore!'

Alf had a sudden thought — what would she do without her ukulele? When she climbed up the steps at the front of the stage, all she was carrying was a shoulder-bag. He was struck by how smart she looked. She had on a nice hat, a new-looking suit, high heels and what seemed to be real silk stockings. Some of the men in the audience gave wolf-whistles.

At the microphone Sonia acknowledged the applause with a smile. 'Thank you, ladies and gentlemen. Thank you, you're very kind. I promise you, I had no idea this was going to happen. However, I feel privileged to be asked to sing to you. And what better song than the one the boys always ask for?

You know it . . . I know it . . . Yes! That's right! . . . "Lili Marlene".' The audience applauded.

A German song! Alf knew the song and thought it was soppy. In this he knew he was out of step with the rest of the world. What puzzled him more than the words and music, was the fact that it was *German*. How could we even think of liking one of *their* songs? Sadly this must prove that Mr Churchill was not perfect. If Alf had been Prime Minister he would have had it banned.

Listening to Sonia singing, he realised she wasn't using her own voice. At least, it wasn't a voice he recognised. Dave used to say she didn't sing, so much as chirp like a bird. Of course they always did comedy numbers. And this wasn't like her old style at all. He tried to think of who she sounded like. Not Vera Lynn — she didn't have that sobbing sound that put Alf's teeth on edge. Really she was most like an American singer, the kind you saw in films. That was it! He was right. The new clothes, the voice — she was just like a film star. When he looked at the audience, he could see they were seeing her in the same way. Even though he didn't like the song, he was very impressed at the way Sonia was putting it across. He'd seen enough good and bad artists on the halls to recognise a great performance when he saw it. She was selling the song with confidence and skill . . . and they were hanging on every word. Alf experienced a mixture of feelings. He was tremendously proud. But at the same time, she seemed unfamiliar. Less like his mom and more like a person he hadn't met before.

She brought the house down. There was as much applause from the performers backstage as the audience. Dot and Amy were ecstatic. They hugged Alf and told him his mom was a star, and how proud he should be. Sonia returned to her seat beside Bill at the front, and the show carried on. Not very well, according to the next turn, a comedy couple from Oldbury. They wanted to know how you could follow *that*? But apart from them, everyone was thrilled that a real pro had consented to appear. *Cinderella* hit the right note, with its knockabout humour and gags about the war. Alf and the girls earned a generous response from the workers. They were breathless with excitement when they lined up with the rest of the company to sing the National Anthem at the end of the evening.

Back in the kitchen Alf got changed as quickly as he could. At that precise moment he was more anxious to find a plate of sausages than meet his mother. But Marge and Else seemed to have disappeared — along with their sausages.

'Hullo Alf,' Sonia put her arm round him and gave him a hug.

She smelled different. He guessed it must be posh scent. 'Mom, have you got anything to eat? I'm starved.'

Sonia laughed and ruffled his hair. 'Now I know I'm back. Hang on a bit.' She opened her shoulder-bag and took out a strange chocolate bar. 'I was going to keep this as a surprise treat for you. But you'd better have it now. Here.'

Alf examined the wrapper. It was called 'Babe Ruth'. He let out a shout. 'Fantastic — it's American!' He tore open the paper and took a bite.

'Nice?' asked Sonia.

He couldn't answer. The taste of the chocolate and its magical filling were beyond words. Alf nodded. He was in heaven.

The dressing area of the kitchen was invaded by relatives and friends and an informal party started. Some of the men had brought bottles of beer and there was a cheer when Dot produced a bottle of sweet sherry. Sonia was whisked away and soon became the focus of attention. Everybody wanted to know about her tour and the well-known names she was working with in ENSA. She told her stories with the same self-assurance she'd shown on stage.

Bill avoided the main cluster around Sonia and found a seat beside Alf. 'Looks like your mom is quite a star now.'

Alf didn't reply. He was too occupied holding the Babe Ruth wrapper up to his nose and sniffing as hard as he could.

'What are you doing?' asked Bill.

'Mom gave me this smashing American chocolate bar. But it's all gone now. If only I'd kept a bit, I'd still have some more to eat.'

Bill grinned. 'They call it candy, the Yanks. They get loads of it. They were like a lot of kids in Italy. Eating that stuff and chewing gum.'

'Did you bring any back?' asked Alf hopefully.

'Sorry mate.'

'Why do they have everything and we've got nothing?'

'Because we've been at war two years longer than them. They didn't come in till they knew which side was going to win.'

'I thought it was because they didn't like Hitler either.'

'That's what they say.'

Alf gave his wrapper another great sniff. 'Well, I'm glad they did anyway.'

The party chatter and shrieks of laughter grew louder. Alf felt tired and wondered when they would ever get home. Needless to say the girls loved a party and wouldn't be shifted until the end. He'd lost sight of his mother.

'Well, I'll be blowed!' exclaimed Bill. 'Look what I see.'

An American soldier had come in and was edging his way around the crowd. He stopped by the two of them.

'Hi. Am I in the right place? I'm looking for a friend of mine — Sonia.'

'Who did you say?' asked Bill.

'Sonia. Sonia Dugmore. Would you happen to know her?'

Bill got up awkwardly and took Alf by the arm. 'Come on. We're leaving.'

'Did I say something?' asked the American.

6

'Well, he's got to stay *somewhere*,' said Sonia's voice. It came clearly through the glass tumbler Alf was holding up to the wall that separated his room from the flat. He'd seen the tumbler idea in a film. You dampened the inside, held it against a wall, and miraculously you could hear what people were saying on the other side.

'Apart from anything else, there's not enough room,' replied Dot's voice.

'Yes there is.'

Sonia and the girls were arguing about the American. His name was Lee and Sonia had met him when she was performing at an American camp.

'You can't expect us just to close our eyes, you know, Sonia.'

'What do you mean?'

'Oh, come on. You're a married woman. Married to my cousin, as a matter of fact.'

Sonia's reply came through loud and clear. She must have been shouting. 'I've *told* you. He's just a boy who's homesick. I felt sorry for him and told him he could come and take pot luck with us. I'd like to think somebody might do the same for Dave.'

'A married woman?'

'Why not?' asked Sonia.

'You *know* why not.'

'You think I'm carrying on behind Dave's back, don't you? Well?'

'You know it's what people will think.'

'People can think what they like.'

Alf knew what the girls were getting at. Gossip about servicemen's wives 'going off' with Americans was common. He'd heard Granny Dugmore say how they would be punished for their sins. Which probably meant they would go to hell. The puzzling thing about that was, if people knew that's what would happen to them, then why did they do it? He wouldn't do *anything* if it meant being dumped into everlasting fire and being tormented by devils. He was sure his mother wouldn't be so stupid either. You'd have to be really mad not to worry about something like that.

He heard Sonia's voice again. 'Look, I can't leave him outside any longer. What must he be thinking? There's me telling him what good friends you are, and what a nice time we'll have over Christmas. He was thrilled when I asked him. And he's brought lots of food and drink. I think he said he put some nylons in as well.'

Alf wanted to bang on the wall and tell Dot and Amy not to be so daft. Dot's voice broke the silence. 'Well, I suppose it *is* Christmas. What d'you think Ame?'

'Seeing he's gone to all that bother. Be a pity to waste everything.'

'He could sleep in Alf's room,' said Sonia.

'Does he know about Alf?'

'What do you mean?'

'. . . Well, you know, that you've got a son?'

Sonia raised her voice again. 'Of course he does!'

'I was only asking.'

Alf mouthed a silent Yippee and got into his pyjamas. He put the light out and climbed up the ladder into bed. There was comings and goings up and down the entry. And before long there was a knock on his door.

'Are you asleep Alf?'

'Yes. But you can come in. The light's out.'

Sonia and Lee came in and she put the light on. Alf pretended he'd just woken up and shielded his eyes. 'Is it an air-raid?' he asked in a sleepy voice.

'No, no,' said Sonia. 'I want you to meet someone. A friend of mine. This is Lee.'

'Hi, Alf.'

Alf sat up. He couldn't help noticing Lee's enormous kitbag. If it had been in a comic, it would have had lines drawn round it to make it look as if it was glowing. 'Hullo.'

'Lee's going to be staying for a few days,' his mother told him. 'We thought he could sleep in here with you.'

Lee smiled and looked at Alf on top of his pile of mattresses. 'That's one heck of a bed you've got there feller.'

'It's the highest bed in England,' said Alf.

'No kidding?'

Sonia and Lee borrowed one of Alf's mattresses and made up a bed in the stage area. Meanwhile Alf quickly wrote a notice and stuck it on one of the wardrobes. It said LEE.

'That's for you,' he told the American. 'You can unpack your kitbag and put your things in there.'

'Thanks Alf. That's real kind. But I guess I'll unpack in the morning. I'm pooped.'

Sonia gave Alf a hug. 'That was very thoughtful of you,' she said with a twinkle in her eye. 'Night, night. Sleep well both of you.'

After she had gone Lee sat on his bed and yawned. 'I saw you at the factory. Who was that guy you were with?'

'My Uncle Bill. He's my dad's brother.'

'Oh. I guess that figures.'

'What?'

'It doesn't matter. Say, this is a great billet,' said Lee, taking in all the furniture and Alf's pictures.

'I guess old Hitler did you a favour, bombing the furniture store.'

'Have you ever been to Hollywood?'

'No. I bet you know more about the place than I do.'

'New York?'

Lee grinned and shook his head. 'Sorry. I just live in a small town nobody ever heard of. Oak Park, Illinois.'

'Where's that?'

'Well, the nearest place you might have heard of is Chicago. It's just a few miles away.'

Chicago! 'You've really been there?'

'Chicago? Sure, lots of times.'

Alf had lost count of the gangster films he'd seen. But they usually took place in Chicago. When they were on the halls, his mom and dad used to take him to the pictures every Saturday afternoon. It was a treat that never failed to thrill him.

'Have you seen any gangsters?' he asked. In his mind's eye seeing James Cagney blasting away at the cops with a tommy-gun.

Lee regarded Alf seriously. 'You know Alf, I think I'm going to have to move out. I guess I'm the dullest guy you'll ever meet. I haven't ever seen a gangster. Except in the movies, like you. Sorry.'

Alf shrugged. 'That's all right.'

'Fact is, back home, we're not much different from you folks here.'

Alf knew that was a daft thing to say, though he didn't mention it. Maybe Lee was meaning to be kind and not wanting to show off. But everybody knew Americans had big cars, posh clothes, and lots to eat. And their policemen had guns. And their chewing gum was in long slim pieces, and not in scrubby little packets like ours.

Lee continued. 'There's one difference I notice over here. The country seems smaller. You know your

79

farms have got those little fields? Back home the farms stretch for thousands of acres. We got space I guess. Out in the mid-west, the prairie lands just seem to go on forever.'

'Prairie' and 'West' meant only one thing to Alf.

'Do you know any cowboys?' he asked.

'Alf, I don't know how to tell you this, but . . .'

Alf shook his head, and Lee nodded. 'You got it. Mostly they grow corn in my part of the country. When I travel down to Missouri to my Uncle Duane's, there's nothing but corn for hundreds of miles. Tell you what we *do* have in Chicago — stockyards. That's where they bring cattle for sale. I guess there must be guys working there who're *like* cowboys.' He gave a heavy sigh. 'Oh boy. The movies sure make life difficult. Everybody over here's got this crazy idea of what we're like.' He took out a packet of gum. Alf's heart missed a beat. 'Want a stick of gum?'

Alf took the gum. It was in a yellow wrapper and it was called Juicy Fruit. The smell was superb, even before he took it out. It *was* fruity! When he started to chew, Lee's dull life in America faded into insignificance as he tasted the gum's incredible flavour. He forgot about gangsters and cowboys. Any place that could make gum like this must be brilliant.

'I guess I'm going to turn in,' said Lee. 'Where's the bathroom?'

'We haven't got one. You have to wash in the kitchen in the flat.'

'I got it,' said Lee, picking up his sponge bag. 'What about the john?'

Alf looked blank.

'The can,' Lee explained. 'The restroom.'

A distant memory from a film helped Alf to understand what Lee was asking. He giggled to himself at the idea of describing their lavatory like that. It was a shed in the back yard. The girls called it the Black Hole of Calcutta. He gave Lee directions and silently wished him good luck on his journey in the pitch dark.

Alf lay back on his bed. He'd got loads of questions to ask when Lee returned. He was still thinking of them when he fell asleep.

By the afternoon of Christmas Day Alf had the bellyache. Of all the rotten things that could have happened, he was sure this was the worst. Since his arrival, Lee had provided a variety of American food and drink. And, of course, Alf had tried everything. His first taste of Coca Cola made him want to leap for joy. But now, he was trying hard *not* to remember all the different things he'd had. Their memory made him feel worse. The tinned turkey had been the best — or the worst, as it now seemed. Its taste would not stop coming back to him. He couldn't even face sucking a peppermint Lifesaver. He looked sadly at the packet and groaned.

They were sitting in the flat, with the remains of Christmas dinner on the table. Lee was between Dot and Amy on the settee, and Sonia was dozing in an armchair.

'Shut up, Alf,' said Dot. 'It serves you right.'

'It's not fair.'

'Here, you can have my paper hat,' Amy said to him. He turned away from her in disgust. What did they think he was, an infant?

Lee spoke. 'Sonia was telling me you two are in show business as well.' Dot and Amy glowed. 'That makes me the odd one out here. What was this pantomime Alf mentioned to me? I don't think we have anything like that at home.'

'Well, it's sort of traditional. At Christmas time,' said Dot.

'It's a kind of fairy story with magic and that,' added Amy.

'So it's for kids?'

'Oh no.'

'It is a bit, Dot.'

'I know,' she replied, 'but if we tell him that, he'll get the wrong end of the stick.'

'I s'pose you're right.'

Dot continued. 'Anyway, there's singing and dancing, and lots of gags. Pretty costumes and a transformation scene. Then there's what we call the Dame. She's supposed to be funny and she's always played by a man. And of course, there's the Principal Boy. He's always played by a girl.'

'With nice legs,' put in Amy.

'Wouldn't it make more sense for the women to be women, and the men to be men?' asked Lee.

Dot took a deep breath. 'No, like I said, it's traditional.'

'And that means you have to turn everything round? Well, I never knew that. That's tough. We sure don't have anything like that.'

'Nobody *minds*,' said Amy. 'It's always been like that. The audience wouldn't go if it wasn't. They'd know it wouldn't be any good.'

Lee thought for a moment. 'I can't figure this out. You did this *Cinderella* . . .'

'That's not the same.'

'It's *not* a pantomime?' asked Lee.

'Yes, it *is*. Just like I explained. Only different.'

'You see, the main girl, *is* a girl — that's Cinderella.'

'But Alf was Cinderella,' said Lee. 'And he's a boy.'

Dot and Amy looked at each other. Amy spoke. 'That's because we didn't have a girl. One of us couldn't have done it.'

'Why was that?' asked Lee.

'Because we had to be men.'

'. . . Oh.'

'. . . Pretending to be women,' added Dot helpfully.

Lee looked at the girls in turn and laughed. 'You're putting me on!'

'If you haven't seen a panto, you'll never understand it,' said Sonia, stretching in her chair. 'How would you spend Christmas at home, Lee?'

'We always go to my Grandma Shultz for Christmas dinner.'

Alf sat up. 'That's a German name, Shultz.'

'Sure. She is German. Leastways she *was*, when she and Grandpa came to the States.'

'What does she think about you coming to fight the Germans?'

'Alf . . .' said Sonia in a disapproving voice.

'As far as Grandma is concerned, I'm here to fight the Nazis. And that's okay by her. She thinks they stink. Like you do. She wants us to get rid of them so Germany can be a decent country again.'

'Just think — having a rotten name like that,' said Alf, pulling a face.

'That's enough,' snapped Sonia. 'That's very rude.'

'You see Alf, most of the people in the US originally came from Europe. In and around Chicago there's lots of different groups. Poles, Swedes, Irish, German, Italian . . .'

'Al Capone, the gangster. He's Italian,' said Alf.

Lee smiled. 'We got good guys as well.'

'There used to be an Italian fish and chip shop in Smethwick, before the war,' said Amy.

'I guess when I was a kid I heard more German spoken than English.'

'Say something in German,' Alf said to Lee.

'Alf, you're being boring,' said Sonia.

'Okay. *Ich werde Märchenkommödie nie verstehen, und Alf hat Magensschmerzen,*'

'What does it mean?' Alf asked.

'It means — "I'll never understand pantomime and Alf's got a sore belly!"' Lee told him.

They all laughed except Alf.

'Come on,' said Dot getting up. 'It's time for charades.'

Alf gave an exaggerated groan. 'Oh no . . .'

'All right, you sit there and be miserable,' said Sonia. 'But if you don't do it quietly, you can go to your room.'

Alf loved charades. He would have liked to join in more than anything. It wasn't the bellyache that stopped him. Sometimes the urge to be different from everybody else and contradict them overcame him. The strange thing was he could *see* himself being awkward. It was as though another force had taken over and it was *it,* rather than himself, that was in charge. Maybe that was how you felt when you'd been hypnotised. He would find himself sneering at people. Like now. Everything they were doing was stupid. And the more they laughed and enjoyed themselves, the worse they appeared. People really got him down when he was in this mood. He supposed that was why he liked films and stories so much. You knew where you were with the people in them. Real people weren't half as good. Why did you get like that when you grew up? He couldn't see himself growing up like that. He wouldn't let it happen.

He studied Lee. He was twenty-one years old and had left college to join the army. Alf had seen Mickey Rooney in a film about being in college. *They'd* worn jerseys with big letters on them and stupid hats. Though *of course,* Lee would tell him it wasn't really like that. For an American, he didn't seem to know much about America. Most of the time he was telling Alf the films he saw were all wrong. Alf couldn't believe that. They were *made* in America, weren't they? How did his mother come to meet *him*? When you thought of all the other Americans. There must be lots who knew more about America than Lee.

Dot and Amy were acting the first syllable of the word 'Churchill'. They had tried miming a steeple and praying, but the other two hadn't got it. They now put on sanctimonious expressions and blessed an imaginary congregation.

'Vicar.'

'Bishop.'

'Bless.'

'Abbey.'

The girls indicated they were getting warm.

'Church!' cried Lee.

For 'hill' Dot and Amy peered upwards and started to climb. Carried away by their act, they climbed over the settee and chairs, wiping sweat from their brows as if tackling Everest.

'Mountain.'

'Climb.'

'The Marx Brothers,' said Lee. The girls stuck out their tongues.

'Hill!' said Sonia. She and Lee congratulated each other and set about acting 'Air-raid'. For 'air' they did deep-breathing exercises, tried to float like fairies, and blew up balloons, before Dot and Amy got it. Their first attempt at 'raid' involved miming commandos, but this failed.

'I know what we can do,' said Sonia. She whispered to Lee. They looked up and put their hands over their ears. Next, Lee put his arm round Sonia's shoulder and they crouched down.

The door opened and Bill came in. He stood leaning on his walking stick and took in the scene. They could see that he was drunk. He let the carrier bag he was holding slide down to the floor. There was a clink of bottles.

With one mind Dot and Amy moved to him.

'Happy Christmas, Bill.'

'Come on in. We were just going to put the kettle on.'

Sonia and Lee stood up. Bill continued to regard them as the girls steered him to a chair and sat him down.

'Bill, this is Lee,' said Sonia.

'Hi,' said Lee.

Bill said nothing.

Sonia turned to Lee. 'Bill's . . .'

'I know, Dave's brother. How you doing, Bill?' he offered his hand. Bill didn't respond.

'Did you have your dinner with your mom and Uncle Charlie?' asked Dot.

Bill nodded. 'They'm asleep. I went down the pub.'

'So we see,' said Amy, picking up his bag.

'What d'you mean?'

'She's just ribbing you,' replied Dot, glowering at Amy.

'There's nothing wrong in having a drink,' declared Bill.

Sonia stepped towards him. 'She wasn't saying that.'

Bill ignored her. 'Where's our Alf? Come here son.'

Alf went to his side. 'Hullo, Uncle Bill.' He could smell the drink on his uncle's breath.

Before he knew what was happening, Bill gave him a hug. It seemed to go on forever. 'How's me old mate, then? Here, I've got your Christmas present.' Bill let him go and gave him a small package. 'Go on, open it.' Alf did so. It was a penknife, just like the one he'd seen his uncle use.

'Oh smashing. Thanks Uncle. Look Mom.'

'Give it us here,' said Bill, taking the penknife back. He pulled out its bottle-cap opener and gave it back to Alf. 'Here, you can try it out. Open us up one of them bottles of beer,' he said, pointing at his bag.

Dot spoke up brightly. 'We were just going to have a cup of tea.'

'I'm not stopping you,' Bill told her.

Alf had difficulty in getting the opener properly located on the bottle-cap. Lee knelt down beside him to help.

'Leave him alone,' said Bill. 'He can do it. He don't

need you. Come on Alf — you show 'em.' He slapped Alf on the back.

'Look, just let me hold the bottle still, okay?' Lee said to Alf. 'There, now you'll do it.'

Alf levered the opener upwards and he felt the cap move. He applied more force. The cap came off suddenly and the bottle slipped out of Lee's hands. Beer spilled over the floor.

Dot quickly rescued the bottle and thrust it into Bill's hand. 'There, I hope you enjoy it.'

'Gosh, I'm sorry.' Amy waved away Lee's apologies and mopped up.

''s typical that. The Yanks step in and muck everything up,' said Bill, taking a swig from his bottle.

'Knock it off,' Dot answered him.

'Is this your knife, Uncle?' asked Alf.

Bill nodded. 'I could see you fancied it the other day.'

'It's smashing. Can I really keep it?'

'Course you can,' said Bill. 'I've give it you.'

'Mom, I can keep it,' said Alf.

Sonia smiled at Alf. 'It's very kind of Uncle Bill.' She spoke to her brother-in-law. 'Are you sure, Bill?' Once more he avoided speaking to her.

'Bet you haven't seen a knife like that one, Yank.' Lee stayed silent. 'No, I bet you haven't. I got it from a German. I bet you haven't seen many of *them* either.' He smirked. 'He was dead at the time, so I got it cheap.' He laughed and took another drink.

Sonia spoke again. 'How's your leg today?' There was no reply. 'I said, how's your leg, Bill?' There was an edge to her voice.

He looked up at her. 'What's it to you?' he asked.

'You seem to be set on ruining our Christmas,' Sonia replied. 'Being friendly seems to have gone out of fashion all of a sudden.'

'Fancy that.'

'So what's your idea? To stop here and get even more drunk, or what?'

'I'm not drunk.'

'You stink of drink,' Sonia told him.

'It's Christmas,' Bill retorted.

Dot interrupted. 'Tell you what, Sonia, we'll do the washing-up and make a cup of tea.'

'I'm friendly,' Bill went on. 'There's nothing wrong with me. But it seems to me, *some* of us have been *too* friendly. Too friendly by half.'

Before she could reply, Dot took Sonia aside and spoke to her quietly. 'Don't upset yourself. The way he's going on, he'll be asleep soon. Just let him be. He'll never believe you anyway.' Sonia protested. 'Not when he's like this, he won't,' said Dot. 'Come on, we'll clear up.'

The women cleared the table and started washing-up in the kitchen. Alf could see that Lee felt uncomfortable and he wished his uncle would stop drinking. He hated seeing him drunk. It made him look stupid. On top of which, you didn't know what he might say or do, and this unsettled everybody.

Bill put on a secretive look and winked. 'Hey, Alfredo, I got something else for you. Come here.' He pressed three pound notes into Alf's hand. 'I sold them screws and things. How about that?'

'That's terrific. Thanks Uncle.'

'I don't think you'd better tell anybody, just in case.' He nudged Alf and gave another exaggerated wink.

'I won't,' said Alf. 'I promise.'

Bill took Alf's arm. 'You stay here beside me. We got to stick together, you and me. Right, Alf?' Alf nodded. 'Not half we haven't. We British gotta stick together. Want a drop o' beer?'

'No thanks, Uncle.' He tried to avoid Bill's breath.

'Go on,' Bill insisted. 'Do you good.'

'No, I've got a sore belly.'

'Drop o' beer make it better. Here.' He gave the bottle to Alf.

'That's not a good idea, Bill,' said Lee.

'Who asked you?'

'I'm just saying, is all. He's only a kid.'

'Well, you can keep out of it,' Bill told him.

'Not if you do that I can't,' Lee replied.

'Oh yes you can. Who the hell d'you think you are?'

'Don't drink it Alf,' said Lee.

Alf didn't want to drink the beer. On the other hand, he didn't want to offend his uncle either. Bill had been very kind to him. And there was the worrying question of what he might do if he refused. The smell of the beer was awful and Alf felt his stomach heave. He was sure he would be sick if he drank it. Alf put the bottle to his lips and tilted it up. As he did so, he stuck his tongue into the bottle's narrow opening, and pretended to drink. He felt the beer's bitter taste on the tip of his tongue, but he didn't swallow a drop.

Lee snatched the bottle away from him and spoke to Bill. 'You damned fool.'

With a tremendous effort, Bill pulled himself up from his chair and faced Lee unsteadily. 'Don't you call me a fool.'

'That was a stupid thing to do.'

'Nobody talks to me like that.'

'Sit down. You're drunk.'

'And I don't take orders from Yanks.'

'Aw, shut up.' Lee turned away from him.

Bill grabbed Lee's shoulder and twisted him round. 'Listen to me, you. You lot think you know everything.'

'Here we go again,' said Lee with a sigh. 'Look pal, I wouldn't argue with you even if you were sober. I know the whole routine. We come over here — we're loaded with dough — we take your girls —

and we can't fight. Right? So you can save your breath.'

'Think you're smart, don't you? said Bill. His face was red and he was breathing heavily.

'Relax. It's Christmas. Have a good time.' There was a hint of a smile on Lee's face which infuriated Bill.

'Just you watch it,' he said through his teeth.

Alf realised that he was probably going to see a fight. A real one, for the first time ever. He had the feeling he should do something. Run into the kitchen and tell them what was going on. But he did nothing. He was much too interested in seeing what happened.

Lee spoke to Bill. 'Buddy, you've had too much. Cool down.'

Lee's tone of voice affected Bill worse than a slap in the face. He put up his fists and Lee laughed at him.

'Come on,' cried Bill, waving his fists. 'I'll show you nobody orders me around.'

'This is ridiculous,' Lee protested.

'Come on Yank.'

'Get hold of yourself, for Pete's sake.'

'Put 'em up.'

Lee shook his head in amazement. Bill took a swing at him and would have connected, if Lee hadn't stepped back.

'Okay. You've made your point,' said Lee. 'Now sit down before you harm yourself.'

'You're the one whose going to get harmed.' Bill's breath was now coming in snorts. He took an awkward step towards Lee. 'Get your fists up. What sort of man d'you call yourself.'

'How many times do you want telling? I'm not going to fight.'

'You frightened, Yank?'

'No, I'm not.'

'See that, Alf?' said Bill. 'Your mom's fancy man is a coward.'

Lee shook his head. 'No, I'm just sorry for you.'

'Right, that does it.' Bill threw an unsteady punch and hit Lee in the chest. Lee took the blow, but did nothing to defend himself. 'Come on — fight!' cried Bill.

Bill's shout brought Sonia in from the kitchen. She yelled at him, but it made no difference. He pivoted himself round on his wounded leg and aimed a punch at Lee's head. It caught the American on the side of the chin, and Lee went down, landing at Sonia's feet.

'That was for Dave!' said Bill.

He stayed on his feet, his eyes ablaze. But his moment of glory was brief. Triumph swiftly turned into agony, as a spasm of pain shot up his injured leg. He staggered and fell onto the settee, sweat running down his face.

Under Amy's supervision, the women attended to the two men. Alf stopped listening to what they were saying. They were all speaking at once anyway. He sat in a corner and opened his Lifesavers, desperate for something to take away the taste of the beer. It hadn't been a fight after all. Lee hadn't done anything. He'd just stood there and let Bill hit him. Maybe he didn't want to fight because of Bill's wounded leg. But he didn't need to let himself get hit, all the same.

Amy declared the best treatment for Bill's leg was rest, so he was put into Lee's bed. and after a few aspirins he soon fell into a deep sleep. Lee looked worse than he felt. He had a split lip and his cheek was swollen. However, he said he wasn't in any pain, and eventually persuaded them to stop fussing over him.

Before long they had their cup of tea.

'Thank heavens for that,' said Dot. 'I couldn't manage without my cuppa.'

'Could I have some more milk in mine?' asked Lee. 'It's still a little hot, with my lip and all.'

'Lee, I just don't know what to say . . .' said Sonia.

'I've told you. It's okay. Forget it ever happened.'

'It wasn't your fault, Sonia,' said Dot.

'Lee,' asked Alf, 'why didn't you move out of the way? When Uncle Bill punched you?'

'I guess I forgot to.'

'You could have, easy,' said Alf.

'Yeah, well I'm dumb.'

'That'll do Alf,' said Sonia. She spoke to Lee. 'I wish you had though.'

'Well, I was going to. But when I saw you come in, I guess I got distracted. The next thing I knew, he'd got me.'

Dot and Amy worked hard at getting the party going again. They told jokes, solved silly riddles, and played guessing games. Then it occurred to the girls that everyone had contributed except Alf.

'Come on, Alf. It's time you thought of something.'

'I don't know any games,' he told them.

'Well, what about tricks?'

'I got one,' said Lee. 'Give me that empty beer bottle, Alf.' He took a sixpence from his pocket, wet it with beer, and placed it on the opening in the neck of the bottle. He then wrapped his hands around the neck of the bottle, to warm it. Within a few moments the coin began to lift up and down. They applauded.

'I can think of one trick,' said Alf. 'It's not very good. But it works.' He got a glass tumbler from the kitchen and dampened the inside under the tap. He held it up to the wall. 'If you hold your ear to it, you can hear what's on the other side.'

'That's no good,' said Amy. 'There's only Bill through there and he's asleep.'

'Listen,' said Alf.

They took turns with the tumbler, and they heard Bill snoring as clearly as if he were in the room beside them.

'That's a great trick,' said Lee.

The three women exchanged glances, and then looked at Alf.

'Well,' said Sonia. 'Fancy that.'

7

Alf was bitterly jealous when Sonia and Lee were preparing to leave after Christmas.

'Why can't I come?' he'd wanted to know.

Sonia sighed impatiently and explained yet again. 'I'm going on tour and it would be impossible,' she told him.

'It wasn't when we were with dad,' said Alf.

'That was different. I've told you. We do one-night stands.'

'I could do an act,' he suggested.

'ENSA doesn't employ juveniles,' replied his mother. 'Now please stop going on about it. You will be far happier here.'

'No I won't.'

Lee had been packing his kitbag during this and he stood up and spoke to Alf. 'Well, what do you know! Look what I just found — a Babe Ruth candy bar. Think you could find a home for it, Alf?'

Alf was blowed if they were going to get round him like that and shook his head.

'Come on feller,' said Lee. 'I can get more back at the camp.'

'Where are your manners, Alf?' said Sonia. 'Say thank you to Lee.'

Alf picked up the chocolate bar and threw it in the fire. Deaf to his mother's anger, he watched it sizzle in the flames and sniffed its sickly smell. It was a sacrifice. But it was the only way he could think of to show his mother how unfair she was being.

When he looked back on her visit, she was like a different person to him. It was more than her new clothes and perfume. Something about her had changed. She seemed to have forgotten the jokes and silly stories they used to share, and how they could always make each other laugh. She'd been anxious that he was happy living with Dot and getting on well at school. But she'd sounded more like an unfamiliar aunt than his mother.

When he went back to school in January he discovered that Sonia was being regarded as something of a celebrity. The local paper had printed an article about her performing with ENSA and her guest appearance at the works concert. Even the teachers remarked about her success and Alf had no choice but to put on a cheerful face and hide his real feelings. Deep inside him, however, was the fearful suspicion that his mother had abandoned him for another life.

As the dreary days of winter dragged on, he started to become more involved in his school work and began to earn Mrs Kenrick's praise. He was sure there was an understanding between them and, ignoring the jibes he got from the other boys, he determined to become her star pupil.

He was helped in this ambition by Mrs Kenrick herself. She held the belief that as a skill, talking was more important than writing. This gave Alf a head start on all the others. Not only was he a confident speaker, his experience in the music hall gave him a rich fund of material to talk about. He looked forward to their daily 'talking time', which always followed afternoon playtime. Secretly he was glad most of the class disliked having to stand up and speak.

One cold afternoon in February, with the pipes hardly on and everybody wrapped up in their overcoats, Mrs Kenrick addressed her class.

'Whatever you children end up doing in this life, you will use spoken language far more than written.

Whether you become a dustman, or a professor. A nursemaid, or a duchess. Any occupation you can think of.'

'A policeman, Miss . . .'

'A soldier . . .'

'A sailor . . .'

'The Prime Minister, Miss.'

'Mr Churchill's a very good example of what I mean,' she told them. 'Can you imagine the state the country would be in if the Prime Minister couldn't speak very well?'

'. . . Please Miss, he's posh.'

She started the talking time by calling Alf forward and some of the class cheered, knowing they would be sure of a laugh. However, instead of asking Alf what he would like to talk about, she asked Audrey to come up as well and explained what she wanted them to do.

'We're going to try something different today. Let's pretend Alf and Audrey are on the wireless. She's going to be a famous person and Alf will talk to her, and ask her questions about herself. Who would you like to be, Audrey?'

'Dunno, Miss.'

'I'm sure you can think of someone.'

Audrey shuffled awkwardly and shook her head.

'Who could Audrey be?' The class called out names and Mrs Kenrick looked hopefully at Audrey.

'I don't know none of them,' she told her.

The class laughed. Mrs Kenrick shushed them with a look.

'Come along Audrey. I'm sure you can try.'

'Not if I don't know who they am,' said Audrey.

'*Are*,' corrected Mrs Kenrick.

'Please Miss,' said Alf. 'She could just be herself and pretend she's famous.'

'That's a good idea. What about that, Audrey?' Mrs Kenrick asked.

The girl gave a reluctant nod.

Alf didn't see this as being at all fair. If his teacher had been anyone other than Mrs Kenrick, he would have protested. He knew what she was up to. She was using him to persuade Audrey to speak. He was supposed to scrap his brilliantly funny talk. He decided he would shine at Audrey's expense and started in great style.

'Good evening ladies and gentlemen. We have a surprise for you tonight. A mystery guest!' The ripple of amusement that went round the class told him he was off on the right foot. 'I'm as much in the dark as you are — as the man said to the lamppost in the blackout!' (That had been one of Dave's regulars.) 'Still, I do know that our guest is famous. Can you tell me your name, please?'

'Audrey.' There were some giggles from the class. '. . . .Audrey Sutton.'

'Now, I believe you're famous Miss Sutton. The trouble is, I've never heard of you. Can you tell us why you're famous?'

Audrey seemed to be studying the floor, but then she started to speak. 'I'm the most famous dancer in the world. I always knew I would be. And now I am. The King's seen me dance. And I've bin to America and danced in a film. I live in London. But I send flowers to me mother. Her lives in Smethwick. When I go back to see her, I give her a kiss. And her says — "My little girl, who would have thought it?" And her wipes a tear away from her eye.'

'Miss Sutton, could you tell me . . .'

'I've got smashing clothes. And they'm all new. And I've got lots of scent. Once I spent twenty pounds in a shop. But I didn't care. Then I had a cup of coffee in a caff. When I come out, I give some money to a poor man.'

The more she went on, the less Alf was able to think of anything to say. She'd taken over and there was nothing he could do about it.

'We never had no money when I was a girl. Never had no nice clothes. Didn't have proper shoes. I had to wear wellies all the time. When nobody was looking, I'd tek them off and dance about. That's when I made up me mind to be a dancer.'

Alf started to speak, but Mrs Kenrick shook her head and hushed him. The class was quiet and everybody seemed to be listening as Audrey went on. She was the centre of attention, standing there in her patched old overcoat that was too large for her, and her wellington boots. It was because of these that the boys had nicknamed her 'Smelly Wellies'.

When Audrey stopped Mrs Kenrick spoke to her. 'How did you become a famous dancer, Miss Sutton?'

She frowned and remained silent.

'We would be very interested to hear.'

'I wished . . . as hard as I could,' she said at last.

'And your wish was granted?' asked Mrs Kenrick.

Audrey nodded and went back to her desk.

The next day it snowed. There was a snowball fight in the playground between the boys and girls. Except for Audrey. She stood by the bike shed and watched. Alf threw a snowball at her. It hit her on the arm, but she didn't respond.

'Come on,' he shouted. 'I'll throw another.'

She just looked at him.

'I *will*.'

His next snowball hit her on the chest. But apart from brushing the snow off her coat, she did nothing. Alf went to her.

'Why don't you throw one back at me?'

'I don't want to,' she told him.

'You're daft.'

'Alf's got a girlfriend! Alf's got a girlfriend!' A group of boys started pelting them. Alf fought back, yelling at Audrey to help. But instead of throwing snowballs, she placed herself in front of him, protecting him from the worst of the attack. The boys taunted him for hiding behind a girl. By the time the bell ended the fight, he was furious with her.

'Why did you do that? I couldn't see to throw.'

Audrey hung her head. 'I can only mek titchy snowballs.'

'Girls are useless,' he said in disgust.

'Look at me coat,' said Audrey.

'It's your own fault. Don't blame me.'

'I was helping you. They didn't hit you very much, did they?'

'I'm not scared of them,' he boasted.

'You'm a show-off.' She stuck her tongue out and ran inside.

As they were the last ones back in, Mrs Kenrick delegated them to do the milk crates at hometime. As was to be expected, they had to put up with more jeers from the boys when they set about collecting the crates from outside each classroom. Alf suffered in silence, but Audrey was having none of it. She amazed Alf by running up to the boys and confronting them. She swore at them and kicked the nearest one hard on the shin. The teasing stopped. On her way back to Alf, she collected her little brother who was waiting by the Infants' door. He occupied himself drinking the dregs from the milk bottles as they piled up the crates by the playground gate.

'Look at him,' said Alf. 'That's disgusting.'

Audrey shrugged.

'He could get a disease or something.'

'I hope it's one that'll put him in the hospital,' Audrey replied. 'I wouldn't have to look after him then.'

'What d'you mean?'

'What d'you think? I'm stuck with him all blinking day. When me mom's not at work, she's down the pub.'

'Have you got a dad?' Alf asked her.

'Went off,' she said with another shrug.

'In the army?'

'Dunno.'

When they had finished, the little boy took hold of Alf's hand. They left school and it started to snow.

'He could do with some gloves,' Alf said to Audrey.

'Think I don't know? It's not my fault we int got nothink.'

The little boy looked up and spoke to Alf. 'Our Aud goes on about you.'

'Shut up Harry,' snapped Audrey.

''er says you'm smashing,' said her brother with a grin.

Before Audrey could respond, she was hit in the face by a snowball. The boys had been waiting and began pelting them as soon as they came in sight. Caught by surprise they could hardly defend themselves and got a thorough pounding. The gang ran off shouting 'Smelly Wellies!' Harry was on his knees in tears. Alf picked him up and tried to brush the snow off him. Audrey had come off the worst. She was covered in snow and a trickle of blood was running from her nose.

'It was because you kicked him,' Alf told her.

'I'll kick him tomorrow an' all,' retorted Audrey.

They trudged on, cold and wet. Harry whimpered as he tried to keep pace, and Audrey wept silently.

'Does your face hurt?' Alf asked her and she shook her head. 'They've gone now. It'll be all right.'

'It's not *them*. We int got nothing for our tea. Mom don't get her wages till tomorrow. Her said we'd just have to scrat around. Her won't be in.' Audrey sniffed and bit her lip. 'Her don't care.'

Alf knew there were 'bad families'. Most of the adult gossip involved them in one way or another. Parents told their children about them, to make them grateful for coming from a decent home. When youngsters misbehaved, they were told they would end up like the poor kids. The threat usually worked. Nobody was keen to become a grubby outcast. Fortunately for Audrey and Harry, Alf's prejudices were not as deeply rooted as those of his classmates. He'd not been in the area long, and his own family life had been unconventional. It's likely that nobody else in Mrs Kenrick's class would have responded to the present situation as he did.

He stopped on the pavement and spoke to Harry. 'Want some toast?' The boy nodded. 'All right, if you stop crying, you'll get some.' He spoke to Audrey. 'I've got some money. We'll buy a loaf. You can come back with me for a bit if you want.'

She looked at him, as though to check that he really meant it.

'Ta.' She took Harry's hand. 'Hark at me, you. We'm going to Alf's. If you don't behave yourself, you won't get nothink.'

Harry grinned and offered his free hand to Alf.

He lit the fire in his room and borrowed some margarine and jam from the flat. Before long they were sitting warming themselves and eating toast.

'You in 'alf lucky,' said Audrey, for the fifth or sixth time.

'That really your bed Alf?' asked Harry. 'Can I go up the ladder?'

'You be quiet and behave,' ordered his sister.

'You can go up if you want,' Alf replied. 'Take your boots off though.' He looked in one of the dressing-table drawers. 'Here, that's a stick of real American gum.'

'Aud — look what Alf give us!' cried Harry.

'What d'you say then?'

'Ta Alf.' He scrambled up the ladder on to the bed.

Alf felt Audrey staring at him. He poured them

more tea. She'd hardly taken her eyes off him since they'd arrived.

'I can't hardly believe it,' she said.

'What?'

'You being on the stage and that,' she told him.

'Oh, that.' He felt himself blushing.

'Meeting famous people. What's it like?'

'All right.'

'Didn't you never know how lucky you was?' Audrey asked.

'I suppose so,' he replied.

'I'd've bin the happiest person in the world if it'd bin me.'

'It was rotten sometimes,' Alf added.

'Get away.'

'Honest.'

'It couldn't never have bin as rotten as living down our way.'

Alf had to admit that was probably true.

'Can I tek off me wellies?' she asked.

'If you want.'

'They're soaking.' She took them off and put them by the fire. He noticed she wasn't wearing any socks and her feet were dirty. He moved back from the fire a little.

'*Do* you dance?' he asked her.

She shook her head. 'I just pretend I do. When I'm in bed, and *he's* asleep.'

Harry made snoring sounds and giggled.

'Do you want to go on the stage?' said Alf.

'I can't do nothink.'

''er can tell stories,' said Harry.

'Shut up, you,' Audrey called up to him.

''er can an' all,' Harry told Alf.

'I know,' said Alf. 'She did one at school.'

'That wasn't no good,' said Audrey frowning.

'Mrs Kenrick thought it was. What sort of stories do you like to tell?'

Harry spoke up again. 'About having a proper mom and dad. Nice ones and everythink. Go on Aud, tell us one.'

'I've warned you.'

'When did your dad go off?' asked Alf.

'Can't remember. Ages ago. He was a pig. He used to hit us. And me mom.'

'Why?'

'I dunno. 'Cause he didn't like us. We didn't like him neither.'

'My dad's in the army,' said Alf.

'Killing Germans!' shouted Harry, pretending to fire a machine-gun.

'I'll kill *you*, if you don't pipe down. There was a bit in the paper about your mom. Entertaining the troops. What's her do?'

Alf showed her photographs of the act, when they were *Sonia, Dave and Sonny*.

'She in' half pretty, your mom,' Audrey said with a sigh. 'And look at your dad. Dead smart. I bet you don't half miss them.'

She gazed at each glossy print in turn, handling them as though they were precious objects. 'They'm just like film stars.' She pointed at him in his Colour Sergeant Bulldog uniform. 'That don't look like you. All neat and that.'

'I was dressed up.'

'You don't look like that at school,' she said.

'What do you expect? They'd think I was daft.'

'I wouldn't,' she told him.

'Everybody else would,' Alf responded.

'They'm stupid. They don't know nothink about wonderful things. I'd like to shoot the lot of them . . . except Mrs Kenrick.'

'What do you mean — wonderful things?' he asked her.

'Being on the stage. Wearing nice clothes. Looking smashing. Everybody clapping you.'

103

She placed the photographs in a neat pattern on the floor and sat looking at them in silence. Every now and then she adjusted one. Alf began to realise why she had been interested in him. She'd built up a dream world about being on the stage. And here he was, somebody who'd been part of it. Of course, she'd got it all wrong. He knew what being on the stage was *really* like. But he was also sure he wouldn't change her mind, no matter what he said. She wouldn't believe him, if it didn't fit in with her dream. She just wanted to lose herself in the glamour. A bit like him in the films he saw. Maybe for *her,* meeting him, was like *him* meeting James Cagney. He laughed at himself. It was a ridiculous idea. However, a small part of him sensed that it wasn't. It made him feel strange. And for once he didn't want to show off.

'That's beautiful.' Audrey pointed at the dress Sonia was wearing in one of the pictures.

Alf knew his mom had made it out of dyed net and tinsel. But he agreed with Audrey. 'It was her favourite,' he lied.

'It's the nicest. You can tell.'

She looked up suddenly and questioned Alf. 'Did you wear make-up?'

'Yes.'

She giggled.

'You have to,' he told her.

'What's it like?'

'I'll show you. I've got some over here.'

He went to one of the chests of drawers and took out the shoebox in which he kept his make-up. He took off the lid and released its special smell. Audrey's face lit up. Delicately she removed the two cigar boxes containing greasepaints. A larger one for the chunky sticks, a smaller one for the liners.

'Don't it smell nice?' She tried one of the sticks on the back of her hand.

'Do you want to put some on?'

'Could I? Honest?'

He led her to one of the dressing-tables. 'Rub some of that cream on your face and I'll tell you what to do.' He'd seen Sonia make up lots of times, but he had difficulty remembering which sticks she used. Audrey ended up looking much too pink, but she didn't seem to mind. Fortunately there was no problem when it came to lining her eyebrows and putting on eyeshadow. Alf concluded that girls must be born with that sort of skill.

She jumped up. 'Harry — look at me!'

There was silence from the bed. He was asleep.

Alf opened the Cinderella wardrobe and took out the wig he'd worn. He gave it to Audrey. She held it as though it might explode. Slowly she turned back to the mirror and put it on with extreme care. She sank down on the seat and sat looking at herself.

For something to do, Alf put some coal on the fire and turned Audrey's wellies round so they would get properly dry. He tidied up their tea things. Still she sat there staring into the mirror. He gathered kindling, paper and matches from the appropriate wardrobes, and went through to the flat to make up Dot and Amy's fire.

He knew he would be in for a hard time at school. Very few of the boys risked becoming friendly with a girl. That was asking for trouble. Not only that — he'd become friendly with Smelly Wellies! It was difficult to believe. But he just couldn't help himself. The feeling that he wanted to be kind to her and give her things, wouldn't go away. Somehow she made him feel guilty, ashamed of his good fortune. How would he have got on with a cruel father and a drunken mother?

His relationship with his parents was different from other children of his age. He knew that. And he was proud of being more 'grown up' than the rest of his class. What had not occurred to him before was the idea that others might envy him. Indeed at all the schools he'd attended, including Bearwood Road, the boys had been more interested in football and fighting, than somebody who'd been on the music hall. And nothing could compete with collecting shrapnel and cigarette cards. So Audrey's curiosity had come as a genuine surprise. How often he'd imagined himself to be someone special! At last he'd met somebody who really seemed to believe that he was. That should have been brilliant. Instead it placed a responsibility on him — as though he had a debt to repay.

When he returned to his room Audrey was dancing. She was humming to herself and moving gracefully this way and that. Around her waist was the towel they had used to dry themselves. Her eyes were half closed and Alf wasn't sure if she'd noticed him or not. He wound up the old portable gramophone the girls used for rehearsals and put on a waltz from their collection of records.

The music had the opposite effect to the one he'd intended. Audrey froze.

'Don't you like it?' He stopped the gramophone. 'I could put on another.'

She shook her head.

'Well, you need music to dance,' he said.

'I can't dance.'

'You can if you want.'

'I can't,' she replied stubbornly.

'My dad dances,' said Alf. 'He says the trouble with most people is they listen to the music with their head. What you have to do is listen with your body.'

'It's easy for him to talk,' she said.

'I'm going to make some more toast.' He put on the gramophone again and the room filled with music. He kept his back to Audrey as he knelt down in front of the fire with the toasting fork. After a while he knew she was dancing, but he

106

didn't turn round. When he switched the gramo-phone off at the end of the record, she smiled at him. Embarrassed, he spread the toast with marga-rine.

Audrey joined him at the fire. 'Like me frock?'

'Not half. What's it cost? A hundred quid?'

'And the rest.'

'Very posh.'

She took the slice of toast he offered. 'You going back on the music hall after the war?'

'I s'pose so,' he said.

'Don't you want to?'

'I dunno.'

'*I* would,' said Audrey firmly.

'They'll have to alter the act anyway. Mom and dad.'

'Why?'

'Mom's changed,' Alf told her.

'How?'

'Singing like she does. Love stuff and that.'

'And her's famous now,' Audrey went on. 'Being in the paper.'

Alf smiled to himself at what Sonia would have said about being in the *Smethwick Telephone*.

'I think I might be an engineer,' said Alf. 'Make things.'

'What?'

'Machines and things.'

'Work in a factory?' said Audrey scornfully. 'That's what everybody does round here. And look at them.'

What Alf meant was that he was going to be a brilliant inventor. Not work on the factory floor. Other people would do that, making his inventions. But he didn't know how to say it without sounding like a show-off.

He changed the subject.'I've finished my comic if you want it.'

'Ta.' Audrey went to the dressing-table and began to

put away the greasepaints. 'I've never known anybody as kind as you,' she said quietly.

Alf ate his toast and looked in the fire. Her wellies were quite dry now.

And so Audrey and Harry came to Alf's most afternoons after school. During the day Alf and Audrey hardly looked at each other and never spoke. They also left school seperately, to avoid the inevitable jeering had they been seen together. He would spend a few coppers of his money from Uncle Bill and buy some bread or buns. Little Harry soon became convinced that Alf must be a millionaire.

They told stories, Audrey danced, and before long they found themselves acting plays which they made up as they went along. Alf and Audrey revelled in being a whole host of exciting characters. However, Harry became a problem. He always had to be someone small who didn't say very much, or an animal. On the day they told him to be a frog he rebelled.

''S not fair. I'm not playing.'

It was Audrey's idea to act 'being on the music hall'. Once they started they found it was the perfect story. It never stopped. They could be on stage doing an act. In the dressing-room getting ready. Travelling in the train between bookings. In their digs. Even Harry was happy. He became an important part of their word-famous act *Audrey, Alf and 'arry — the Gleeful Threesome*.

'Good morning, madam. Who are you two?'

'Me and 'im.'

'You and him?'

'No, *me* and 'im.'

'I see. What can I do for you?'

'You can tell Mr Churchill, we'm fed up.'

'Fed up? Why's that?'

'You tell 'im 'arry.'

'You can't get nothink. No sweets. Nothink.'

108

'That told him.'

'Just a minute my good lady, don't you know there's a war on?'

'There's nothink we can do about that.'

'Oh yes there is.'

'Oh no there isn't.'

'Oh yes there is.'

'What?'

'You can sing this little song with me.

We're going to Hit Hit Hitler
Where it Hurt Hurt Hurts . . .'

After the song they took their curtain-call. Harry loved bowing and would have carried on forever if Audrey hadn't told him he wouldn't get any chips in the dressing-room. He quickly rushed off and opened his imaginary packet and started tucking into his invisible supper.

Audrey sat at a dressing-table and touched up her make-up. 'The manager should be here soon with our wages.'

Harry jumped off his chair and pretended to knock on the door.

'I wonder who that is, knocking on the door?' Audrey opened the invisible door.

'Yer wages,' said Harry.

'Oh, ta. Our wages my dear.' She handed the money to Alf.

Harry quickly nipped back to his seat as Alf divided the 'money'.

'And that's two bob for you, son.'

'I'm off to buy some sweets.' Harry jumped down from his chair again and went off to his own pretend sweetshop.

'Where are we going to next week?' asked Audrey.

'Er . . . Wolverhampton. Top of the bill.'

'That'll be nice. I'm going to do me new dance,' she told him. 'What about you my dear?'

'I dunno. Maybe I'll do some magic. I think I'll saw Harry in half.'

'That's a good idea. Will you put him together again?'

'Maybe I will,' said Alf. 'There again, maybe I won't.'

They had to stop because they were laughing so much.

'I think I'm going to change my name,' said Audrey.

'Why?'

'Audrey's dead common. I'm going to be Annette. That's lovely. Makes you sound all pretty.'

'All right then, I'll be Mike,' he said.

'Mike? What's so good about that?'

'Makes you sound like you've got muscles,' replied Alf.

As they were clearing up they heard somebody knocking at the flat door. Alf opened his door and called up the entry. It was Grandad Charlie. Immediately he came in, Audrey and Harry became shy and wouldn't speak. As soon as they could they left.

'What they doing here, Alf?' asked Charlie.

'Just playing and stuff.'

'Don't you know who they am? That's the Sutton kids. You want to keep away from that family. They'm tykes. The dad's in prison. And *her* don't look after them. You don't want to go mixing with the likes o' them.'

'What did he do, to get put in prison?' Alf asked him.

'He was a right fly-by-night. Never had no proper job.'

'Did he steal things?'

'So they said,' replied Charlie. 'He broke in the Co-op.'

'What did he take?'

'I dunno. Any road, they give him a chance. Said if he joined up they'd let him off. 'Course he twisted them. Never went near the army. So the next time they nabbed him they put him in the clink.' Charlie shook his head. 'So you keep away from them. If your dad was here, that's what he'd tell you. Just you leave them alone.'

'It's not *their* fault,' said Alf.

'They'm a bad family Alf. You've only got to look at them.'

'You can't help who your mom and dad are.'

'And you can't help growing up like them neither,' Charlie replied.

While Alf was making them a cup of tea, Charlie moved awkwardly round the room, talking about nothing in particular. Normally he would have placed himself in the best armchair by the fire and filled his pipe. Alf knew something was up.

'I've come about your dad and mom. There's bin talk.' Charlie stopped and wondered how to go on.

'What do you mean?' asked Alf.

After a heavy silence, Charlie continued. 'From what we've heard, it looks like your mom's gone off. Her's been carrying on, if you know what I mean. And somebody's wrote to your dad.'

'How do you mean, gone off?' said Alf.

'Like I said, there's bin talk. What with that, and what your Uncle Bill said at Christmas.'

'What was that?'

'Her brought that Yank here,' Charlie went on.

'Lee. He's been sent overseas. She told me in a letter.'

'See, her'd been seeing him.'

'He's nice,' Alf told him.

'That's neither here nor there.'

'Do you think Dad would mind?'

'Course he would,' replied Charlie stiffly.

'Why?'

'You'm too young to understand,' he said. 'Any road, your gran's upset. Her's worried about you.'

111

'Why?' Alf asked again.

'Because you'm her grandson.'

'I'm all right.'

'But *now* . . . now you know what I've just told you and that . . .'

Alf paused and thought. 'I'm still all right.'

Charlie became exasperated. Alf wasn't making his job any easier. 'If you was older, you'd know what I was on about.'

'I know what you mean, Grandad Charlie,' said Alf.

'Well then. It'll be upsetting. So your gran thinks it would be best if you come to live with us.'

'Why?'

'Don't you never say nothing else?' demanded Charlie.

'I was just asking.'

'You shouldn't have to. Because we'm your family, that's why.'

'I'm okay here with Dot and Amy,' Alf told him.

'Your gran thinks her should look after you, for your dad's sake.'

Alf thought quickly. 'But mom's arranged for me to live here. She pays for my keep.'

Charlie sighed. 'I know. But you'm your dad's son. And it's like your mom's cheated him. So it's natural your gran wants to help him, 'cause he can't do nothink. Away in the army.'

'Did dad say I've got to go to gran's?' asked Alf.

'That's what he'd want,' said Charlie.

'But he knows I'm happy here.'

'No, he don't. You've never wrote to him, have you?'

Alf remembered the cheap little Christmas card he'd sent to his dad. His only communication with Dave since he'd been away. If only he'd written something on that. One crummy little sentence would have done. 'These are the best digs in the world.' That's all it would have needed. But he hadn't. And now he could kick himself.

'I'll write to him today,' he told Charlie.

'About time an' all. You int half let him down. The both on you have. You and your mom. Think how he feels. Not knowing nothing, and then this happens.'

'What about mom?'

'What about her?' said Charlie.

'Does she know gran wants me?'

'Your gran wouldn't speak to her. Her'll have a word with Dot.'

The next day after school, Alf went to the post office and asked how to send a telegram.

'You'm a bit young to be sending telegrams.'

'I've got the money,' said Alf.

'Does your mother know?' he was asked.

'It's her I'm sending it to.'

The man became more reasonable. 'Oh well, I s'pose that'll be all right then.'

Alf wrote the address Sonia had given Dot for use in an emergency. It was the ENSA office in London. He knew the message had to be brief, so he settled on: TROUBLE WITH GRAN PLEASE COME. He was going to add HOME, but decided against it.

8

Audrey and Harry were waiting for him when he got back from the post office. Alf gave the little boy some coppers and sent him off to the bakers. There was a letter from his mother lying on the mat when he opened the door. He quickly tore it open.

Dear Alf,

By the time you get this I'll be 'somewhere overseas'!! Sorry I can't tell you where. In fact I don't know where it will be myself! As you can imagine, I'm very excited about going. I certainly hope it's somewhere warm. This winter has been awful. Everywhere we've taken the show seems to have been cold. Thank you for your letter. I'm glad you are liking school. Mrs Kenrick sounds a smashing teacher. I wish I'd had her when I was at school!

I'll write to you as often as I can. Won't be too easy, as we'll be on the move most of the time. As usual we'll be performing in as many camps as we can. If the response is only half as good as it has been in England, we'll be very happy. Troops are a fantastic audience!

Look after yourself.
Lots of love,
Mom.

He threw the letter down and swore. Audrey giggled nervously. But when she saw his frown she asked what the matter was. Alf told her about the trouble between his parents, and his having to live at his gran's.

114

'Won't your mom get your telegram?' she asked.

'Course she won't. Not if she's been sent overseas.'

Audrey put the kettle on. 'What you going to do?'

'I don't know.'

'Have you written to your dad?'

Again Alf frowned and shook his head. 'No, not yet.'

'Why not?' she wanted to know.

'I'm going to,' he snapped back. 'Stop going on about it, will you.'

He got the fire going and she made the tea in silence. The door burst open and Harry rushed in.

'I got the buns. They'm whoppers. Can I 'ave one Aud?'

Audrey took the bag from him. 'Give us them here and be quiet.'

Harry looked at the other two in turn. 'What we going to play?'

'Here.' Audrey gave him a bun. 'Now go outside and play. We got stuff to talk about you wouldn't understand.'

Harry went out and Audrey poured tea for herself and Alf. He sat moodily in front of the fire.

Eventually Audrey spoke. 'I'll tek Harry off. Give you a bit of peace. So's you can write to your dad.'

'The trouble is, I don't know how to do it,' he said.

'Course you do.'

'Who says?'

'You can do it,' she told him. 'You'm clever.'

He gave a long sigh. 'What you don't know is, I've never written to him,' he confessed. 'Not since he's been away.'

'Why not?'

Alf paused before he replied. He'd had the answer on his mind for months, but he'd never said it out loud. 'Because he tried to get out of going into the army.'

Audrey looked puzzled. 'What's wrong with that?'

'You're supposed to go. If you're a man. It's the law. To defend the country and beat the Germans. He didn't want to go because he was a coward.'

'Well, he's in the army *now*, isn't he? What do you want to go on about it for?'

'He was scared,' Alf said.

'Anybody would be,' said Audrey sympathetically. 'Bet you would be. Who wants to get shot at? I thought you liked him — your dad?'

'I did . . . I do,' he admitted. 'He was smashing.'

'Well then, it don't matter.'

Alf tried to find the right words to make her understand. 'Men are supposed to be tough. Everybody knows that.'

Audrey was not impressed. 'My dad was tough and he was a pig,' she said with a snort. 'He just bashed people about.'

'That's different,' Alf replied impatiently.

'Your dad was kind, wasn't he?'

'Yes, he was, but . . .'

'Mine wasn't,' said Audrey, looking at him.

As she had done before, Audrey stirred his feelings of guilt. He'd had everything, and she'd had nothing. All the same, could a girl understand about men? Men had to have courage. Just being kind wasn't enough.

'I'll tell you something,' said Audrey. 'I bet your dad wants you to write to him.'

'How do *you* know?' he retorted.

'Because he's your dad,' she replied simply. 'In any case, if you don't want to go to your gran's, you're going to *have* to,' she added practically.

'It's not just that. What am I going to say about Mom?'

'Tell him they're lying.'

'What do you mean? Who?'

'Everybody. Them who's said her's gone off with another bloke.'

'How do I know they are lying?' he asked her.

116

'Course they am.'

'Why?'

Audrey answered patiently. 'Cause they'm jealous on her.'

Alf hadn't thought of that. He remembered how everybody had crowded round her at the concert. Maybe some people did envy her.

'But I still don't *know,* for sure,' he said.

She dismissed this. 'Look, it don't matter. You don't want them to split up, do you?' He shook his head. 'Well then, tell him you know the truth.'

Alf looked at her blankly. 'What's that?'

Audrey thought for a moment and then spoke with conviction. 'Tell him, her loves him and nobody else. You've got to. Good parents shouldn't be allowed to split up. That's what I think.'

The next day he got a letter from his dad.

Dear Alf,

I'm sorry to have to be writing to you like this. Things haven't been too good between your mom and me. I was never happy at her leaving you and going off into ENSA. I thought it wasn't fair on you, and I still don't. I think she should have made her first job looking after you. Anyway, she saw it differently.

From what I hear she's made other friends. It seems she's gone off and left you and me to get on with it. Not so easy with me stuck here in Haywards Heath and you in Smethwick. So I've asked gran if she will look after you. It would be better if you were there. Dot and Amy don't have much time and I don't think it's fair to expect them to put you up. It was okay when mom was there. But all that's changed. In any case, I know Gran would really like to have you.

So I want you to move to gran's. Remember to

thank Dot and Amy for having you — they've been very kind. Be a good boy at gran's. I know you'll have some fun with Grandad Charlie.

Alf, you and me have got to stick together now. I'll keep in touch as much as I can, and there's a rumour we'll be getting a bit of leave soon. I'm really looking forward to seeing you. I'd like to think you want to see me. See if you can drop me a note telling me we're still mates.

>Love,
>
>Dad.

The second time he read Dave's letter, Alf felt tears in his eyes. Everything had gone wrong. He'd written his own letter, but he'd not sent it because he wanted to copy it out in his best handwriting. Now it as too late. What was the point? He'd got to move to his gran's and that was that. As for his mom . . . It looked as if she really had gone off. Things must have been going wrong for a while. He hadn't known anything about their disagreement over Sonia going into ENSA. He'd thought he was the only one who didn't like it.

Would they get divorced? He knew about divorce — at least, as it was presented in American films. It was always happening there. He didn't know about England. The idea that he might not see his mother again overwhelmed him and he cried. Both his parents had let him down.

But that wasn't how Dot saw it. She blamed Hitler.

'If it hadn't been for the war, there wouldn't have been none of this trouble. They've always had two things in common, your parents. They were devoted to each other, and they're both ambitious. What was your mom supposed to do, when your dad had to go off? Imagine it. One week you're well up the bill in a number-one booking. The next, you're supposed to forget all that, and move in with your mother-in-law. No wonder she couldn't stick it.

Neither would your dad have, if the boot had been on the other foot.'

'Will I be able to see mom again?'

She put her arm round him. 'Course you will. I shouldn't be surprised if everything doesn't turn out all right. When the war's over and we're back to normal.'

Alf thought for a while. 'Dot, mom was really different when she was here at Christmas. And her singing at the concert. She never used to be like that.'

She smiled and shrugged. 'I know. I was that jealous I could've scratched her eyes out! That's what I'm saying, she's talented. Between you, me, and the gatepost, I don't think she really had a chance to shine in the act. You know what your dad was like. He had to be the king-pin. She always had to support him.'

'But she was rotten at the Birmingham Hippodrome,' said Alf.

'Course she was,' Dot agreed. 'She was dropped in at the deep end and didn't have the right material.'

'How did she become so good then?' he asked. 'Suddenly, in ENSA?'

Dot knew that Alf was too bright to be put off by a half-truth. But he was still too young to understand adult relationships. However, she decided to tell him the truth as simply as she could. 'Your mom got the ENSA job because the bloke running the company took a fancy to her.'

'Do you mean he fell in love with her?' he asked.

After the briefest hesitation, Dot plunged on. 'No, no, nothing like that. He *liked* her, and he thought she had possibilities. As a performer. Before the war he was a producer in London. Anyway, he showed her she could go solo. He gave her the confidence she needed.'

'Is he the man she's left dad for?'

'I don't know, Alf. I really don't. I *do* know it's the kind of thing people would say. Outside the company. Things are different in wartime. The company's always together, working hard. Travelling all over the place. They all have to be good friends and get on with each other. Or else it just wouldn't work. And if there's one person who'd understand that better than most, it's your dad.'

'But he says mom *has* gone off,' said Alf. 'Left him.'

There was no soft alternative to what Dot believed to be the truth about Dave. Again she decided not to try to hide it from Alf. 'You know I said I was jealous of your mom? Well, that was a joke. But adults *can* be jealous of each other. Even when they're married. I think that's the trouble with your dad. He's jealous of your mom's success. Before she'd only been what she was because of him. Do you understand what I mean?'

'She's doing well without him.'

Dot nodded. 'That's about the size of it.' She studied Alf, hoping she'd done the right thing. 'Come on, I'll help you pack your stuff.'

Alf bent low over the handlebars of his bike and pedalled as hard as he could. He was favourite to win the road race, just like the ones he'd read about in his dad's old cycling magazines. Granny Dugmore had looked them out. His bike was a second-hand one, done up for him by Grandad Charlie. He didn't worry about the sit-up-and-beg handlebars and lack of gears. In his imagination it was a Claude Butler super-light road racer, and the winner's yellow jersey was as good as his. This afternoon he was completing the mountain section of the 'Tour de France'. He would earn the incredible title of King Of The Mountains. The finishing line was the park gate.

His heroic arrival, to the cheers of thousands, was cut short when he caught sight of the park keeper. He got off his bike and pushed it to a bench. The bike had been the best present he'd ever had. Granny Dugmore and Grandad Charlie had been very kind to him over the last two months. It was a bit like being ill, the way they treated him. And to a certain extent he enjoyed their pampering. However, he still missed his smashing room at Dot's. And he was sure Audrey missed it even more than him, though she didn't say anything. Alf knew she felt sorry for him because of the trouble between his parents. Curiously they'd almost fallen out over that. She was sure he could do something to bring them together. *What*, she didn't know. He was supposed to know because he was clever. She couldn't stand the thought that her dream parents would break up. But he felt helpless. Especially in bed at night when he couldn't stop the tears coming.

He saw Audrey at the gate and waved. She came across to him.

'Where's Harry?' asked Alf.

'They've took him to hospital,' she told him. 'Last night.'

'What's wrong with him?'

'Diphtheria, they think. It was horrible. He couldn't breathe, and sweating and that. I had to go for the doctor meself. Mom was in the pub. The doctor worn't half mad. They sent a policeman to get her.'

'Will he be all right?' said Alf, shaken by the news.

'I dunno. A lady come to the house this morning. Her didn't half go on. About the house and that. Proper bossy. How we was left on our own. Her said we'd be put into care if mom don't buck up her ideas.'

'You mean, put in a home?'

'I think so,' said Audrey.

The very idea struck Alf with terror. To be taken away and put in some institution.

It started to rain. 'Oh no, it's going to pour,' said Alf. 'Where can we go?'

'We can go down home. Mom's at the hospital,' she told him.

He got on the bike first and stood straddling the crossbar. Audrey got on the saddle and they set off, wobbling down the road.

The house shocked Alf. It was in a row of back-to-back houses and it was a slum. He'd heard people talk about slums. Now he knew what they meant. When Audrey let him into the kitchen the first thing to strike him was the awful smell. Immediately he knew he didn't want to touch anything. The table was covered with newspaper to serve as a tablecloth. On it there was an empty milk bottle and an old tin lid of lipstick-stained cigarette ends. The wallpaper was damp and peeling, and in places the lino was completely worn through.

'Home sweet home,' said Audrey.

Alf was speechless. He sat gingerly on the edge of a rickety chair by the table. Audrey put the kettle on. 'I've got some sugar and tea. Hang on.' She went out into the backyard and soon returned with an old biscuit tin. 'I have to hide it from her, for me and Harry. There's a hole in the ceiling of the lav. I stick it in there.'

He noticed a battered toy truck in the corner. 'How long will Harry be in hospital?'

'Dunno. You should've heard the doctor, when I told him Harry didn't have no pyjamas. I told him I didn't have none neither.'

Alf looked at the chipped cup Audrey set before him. For once, his imagination had failed him. He'd often pictured where Audrey lived, but he had never realised it could be as bad as this. It embarrassed him. Now he really knew the difference between them. How he had somehow been picked out and favoured. How she had been left with cruelty and poverty.

'*Might* they put you in a home?' he asked Audrey.

'That's what her said.'

'D'you think that would be better than . . .' He didn't go on. Anywhere would be better than that awful room.

She looked at him as if he'd gone weak in the head. 'Don't be daft. It's horrible being stuck in a home. They cut off your hair and everythink.'

Alf shuddered. 'Why?' he asked.

'Because of the nits of course. Nobody's going to cut off my hair.'

'Maybe your mom will change,' he told her. 'What's happened to Harry must have upset her.'

'Her was crying all right. When the copper brought her back from the pub. Then her was sick. The doctor didn't half give her a row.'

'She's bound to be different now,' said Alf kindly. 'You'll see.'

'Her'd better be,' said Audrey. 'They won't get me in no home,' she added defiantly.

He welcomed the rain as he raced his bike back to his gran's. It felt fresh and clean. Just what he needed after Audrey's house.

Granny Dugmore and Grandad Charlie had already started their tea when he got in.

'Where you been?'

'Riding about.'

'Till this time, in the rain? Look at you. You'm soaked.'

'Sorry, Gran.'

To his relief, they didn't question him about where he'd been. They disapproved of his friendship with Audrey and he knew they hoped it would end. She came from a bad family, and it was sissy to go around with a girl. Charlie had very firm ideas about that. His main reason for giving Alf his bike was the hope that it would provide him with another interest.

Grandad Charlie was excited. The rumours of an Allied invasion of Europe were growing and that afternoon he'd seen a long convoy of lorries. They'd been carrying fighter planes. He'd counted thirty-five. Their wing-tips had been removed and their engine mountings were wrapped in canvas covers.

'You should've seen 'em Alf. Held up the traffic for three parts of an hour.'

'Where were they going to?' asked Alf.

'Down to the south of England,' Charlie told him. 'That's where everything's going now — tanks, planes, guns, men. Everything we'm making in the factory's for the invasion. It can't be long now.'

'You bin saying that for a year,' said Granny Dugmore.

'I'm right though, Glad,' said Charlie. 'Why d'you think Dave's been posted down south to Haywards Heath? It'll be any day now.'

She spoke sharply. 'I don't want to talk about it.'

Alf pricked up his ears and questioned Charlie. 'Is that why dad was moved? To be in the invasion?'

'Now see what you've started,' said Granny Dugmore to Charlie.

'Will he have to fight?' asked Alf.

Charlie glanced at his sister. She got up and went into the back kitchen.

'*Will* he, Grandad Charlie?'

'Well, he is a soldier. Like your Uncle Bill had to.' He gave a quick look at the door. 'Don't say nothing to gran about it though.'

'When will they do it?' Alf went on. 'The invasion?'

Charlie spoke in a whisper, as though wary of enemy spies. 'Word has it, it's going to be the end of May. Or early June. That makes sense. They'll be needing good weather and lots of daylight.'

Demands for a 'Second Front' had been growing for well over a year. Alf had seen numerous cartoons in the newspapers of Mr Churchill being urged by the Russian bear to attack the Continent. The idea was that this would take pressure off the Eastern Front.

How the Allies would ever get enough men and weapons across the Channel to beat the Germans puzzled Alf. Like everyone else, he knew of the so-called Atlantic Wall Hitler had built along the French coast. How did you get through that?

'How will they do it?' said Alf.

'They'll do it, don't you worry.' Charlie shook his fist. 'They'm going to knock old Hitler for six!'

Alf looked at Charlie's grinning face. 'That's what I had to say in the act. The audience always used to cheer.'

'No wonder. It's what everybody wants.'

'Don't the Germans know we're coming? And they've got that big wall. And thousands of guns.'

'And I'll just tell you what *we've* got. We got right on our side.'

'What does that mean?' Alf asked him.

'That we'm right and the Germans are wrong. They'm bad, and they've got to be beat. And they will be. You'll see. Mr Churchill will mek sure of that. And that's another thing. We got the best leaders. Look at the way Montgomery beat them in the desert. At El Alamein.'

'Uncle Bill said a lot of our men got killed there,' said Alf.

'Not half as many as theirs,' replied Charlie. 'You see — we whacked 'em there, and we'll whack 'em in France an' all.'

Granny Dugmore returned. She dropped a thin buff envelope on the table in front of Alf. There was no stamp. It had been franked by the British Forces Post Office. It was addressed to him in his mother's handwriting.

'This come today.' She said no more, and Alf sat looking at the letter.

He didn't know whether he should open it or not. Granny Dugmore poured out their cups of tea and started her knitting. Charlie opened the *Birmingham*

Mail. Alf sipped his hot tea. The knitting needles clicked and Charlie's belly rumbled.

Eventually Alf announced he would go up to his room for his comic. As casually as he could, he picked up the letter and went upstairs. Once in his room he hurriedly opened it.

Dear Alf,

This is the first chance I've had to write to you since I heard that you'd moved to gran's. The first thing I want to say to you is that dad and me both love you. You must remember that, whatever else you might hear. I'm not going to pretend your dad and me haven't fallen out. You're old enough to know that parents sometimes have arguments. The difference with us is, it's happened when we're hundreds of miles apart. The worst thing for me is worrying about you. They'll tell you I've let you down. And maybe I have, in a way. But as you know, we couldn't have stayed together with gran. When we moved to Dot's, it was smashing — wasn't it? We were all happy. And me getting the ENSA job seemed to be part of that. I know you were pleased for me.

I honestly don't know what's going to happen. Dad's fed up, and no wonder. Anyway he's stopped writing to me. But please, *make sure you write to him.* As I say, I know he loves you, and what's happened between him and me won't alter that. We're still your mom and dad, you are our son. Never forget that.

Lots and lots of love,

Mom.

Alf remembered to pick up his comic as he left his bedroom, but he didn't know how he was going to hide his tear-stained face. They would see he'd been crying. However, they wouldn't say anything — it was their way of being kind. Pretending not to notice. In the same way, they never mentioned his mom. As though it would upset him to be reminded that she was still alive. He stopped on the stairs and rested his head against the wall. What he would give to get downstairs and find his mom and dad waiting for him. Just the three of them, like it used to be. He would explain why they had to stay together, and they would smile and agree. His dad would make a joke and his mom would ruffle his hair. Then they'd go off to the theatre and get ready for the show.

He took a deep breath and carried on down. The wireless was on. They were listening to one of Charlie's favourites, Sandy Macpherson at the theatre organ.

'He's just played a tune for somebody in Perry Barr,' Charlie said to Alf. 'I used to go to the dogs there.'

'Another cup of tea, love?' asked Granny Dugmore. Alf shook his head. She smiled at him and pulled his chair in near to the fire. He sat down.

'Want your drawing book?' asked Charlie. 'Here y'are.' He passed Alf his scrapbook and crayons. 'What you going to draw tonight?'

'I don't know.'

Alf emptied his crayons out of their box. He did this in the hope that the red and orange ones would have grown longer overnight. They hadn't. They remained little more than stubs. Whatever he drew, he would have to cut down on explosions and fires — his favourite things to draw. He'd blown up more German tanks and planes than he could remember. He always drew the jagged edges of shell-shattered armour plating so that they emphasised the force of the explosion. This was a trick he'd copied from his comic. Sometimes he would put in a dead body flying through the air.

He started to draw a warship, mainly because he had a practically unused blue crayon that would do for the sea. He added more ships, building up the convoy. Would he put in a U-Boat? No, submarines were not much of a threat any more, thanks to the Royal Navy. He decided the warships would be attacking enemy positions on land. Like it would be in the invasion. He would put the German defences on the right-hand side. That would be the coast of France. As he sketched in the concrete bunkers and their guns, he wondered where he could put the one explosion he had enough red for. Studying the picture as it developed, he realised the enemy gun emplacements looked too big. The Allied convoy appeared to be pathetically small. The thought occurred to him that even if he made the ships larger, their guns would still be smaller than those on land. And the concrete defences would be much harder to destroy than the ships.

'Your dad used to sing this one,' said his gran to Alf.

Alf looked up. Granny Dugmore had paused in her knitting and was humming along with the organ. Charlie was keeping time with his foot. Alf remembered the song well — 'When You're Smiling'. And he remembered what his dad used to say about it: 'One of the greatest songs ever written. Can't fail. Goes down well even if you forget the words. No kidding. It'd cheer them up at a funeral.' Grandad Charlie gave Alf a cheery wink.

Alf returned to his drawing, putting in barbed wire and tank-traps along the beach. Because he wanted the Allies to win, he was tempted to leave gaps in the German defences for our troops to get through. But he knew there wouldn't be gaps. They would have to make them. He drew in some ships close to the shore, with soldiers firing as they clambered out. A way had to be cleared for tanks and equipment. He put in more men, cutting the wire and clearing mines. He hesitated. They were overlooked by a German machine-gun post that he'd drawn earlier. They would be mowed down. It was obvious. *That* could be his explosion. He would have the machine-gun post hit by one of our shells. He worked at it till his red crayon was finished.

But what about the explosions from the big enemy guns? He would have their shells missing the ships and landing in the sea. He quickly drew in splashes. Finished. He sat nibbling the end of his blue crayon, looking at his drawing.

Grandad Charlie looked over Alf's shoulder. 'That's a good picture.'

Alf picked up a black crayon. 'No, it's not. It's rotten.' He methodically started to add lines and shading to the German bunkers, to make them look like cliffs. He added more and more lines, trying to obliterate the guns. But even when they were dense black lumps, he could still see his original drawing underneath. The shape of the guns remained. He couldn't seem to get rid of them.

Mrs Kenrick knew when she was beaten. Her class had been excited all morning and nobody had done any work. She was excited herself. For hours they had heard the rumble of heavy lorries moving tanks and artillery. At the beginning of the afternoon she announced that they would go and watch the convoys. And so she marched her pupils up to Hagley Road singing 'Pack Up Your Troubles In Your Old Kitbag'. Joining the onlookers lined along the pavement, they cheered every vehicle as it went past. The drivers waved back and gave the thumbs-up sign. The crowd was happy and produced an extra cheer when the sun came out. Even the policemen directing the traffic wore large smiles. One cause for amusement were the slogans painted on many of the tanks and trucks. There were crudely daubed pictures of Hitler being hit on the head and kicked on the bottom. Alf noticed one showing the Führer being knocked through the air by a batsman with his cricket bat.

The party atmosphere grew. Adults and children were thrilled by the mighty assault that was now close at hand. At last, the idea of the invasion had become a reality. From all parts of the country, armaments and equipment were heading south for the big day.

'Send us a postcard from Berlin!' Mrs Kenrick shouted to one of the drivers, to the surprise of her class.

'It'll be a pleasure, darling!' came the reply, and she joined in the children's shrieks of laughter.

Audrey grabbed Alf's hand. 'Come on!' She pulled him into the centre of the class group. 'Can we sing a song, Miss?'

'Of course you can! As many as you like!'

They sang 'We're Going To Hit Hit Hitler', just as they had practised it in Alf's room. The class cheered them, and the rest of the crowd urged them to do it again. This time everyone joined in the chorus.

'That was splendid, both of you. Well done!' said Mrs Kenrick. 'Come along, I've got an idea. We're going on tour!' She took the class along the pavement to another spot. Alf and Audrey had to repeat their act. During their third performance, they attracted the attention of a photographer from the *Smethwick Telephone*. He positioned them so that he could photograph them entertaining the crowd as the convoy slowly rolled by in the background.

The vehicles were still passing later in the afternoon when Mrs Kenrick dismissed her class and allowed them to go straight home. Alf and Audrey sat on a garden wall, resting from their efforts. The magic of what they had done still affected Audrey. Her eyes were sparkling and she couldn't sit still. It had been her first-ever public performance.

'They thought we was good!' she shouted over the noise of the trucks. She jumped off the wall and twirled herself round. 'I'm going to go on the music hall and I'll be brilliant! You see. I'll sing and dance and everythink. And I'll have pretty dresses, just like your mom. It'll be wonderful — just you see!'

Alf didn't respond. The excitement had drained out of him. He'd been aware of a growing feeling of fear each time they had sung Dave's song. His dad was going to be part of the invasion and a lot of men were going to be killed. The people watching the convoy knew that, and yet they still cheered and laughed — even Mrs Kenrick. He hated them. His dad could be one of the thousands who would never come back. And tucked in at the back of his mind was the awful knowledge that he had been rotten to his dad. He now understood how Dave must feel, treated badly by both his son and his wife.

Alf had got to tell him it was all a mistake. He'd got to tell him, before it was too late . . .

The road was silent. The last truck had passed by on its way to the south coast.

9

'Tickets, please. All tickets, please.'

Alf and Audrey held their breath as they heard the distant voice of the ticket collector. They were hidden beneath a pile of kitbags and army greatcoats.

'All on travel warrants, lads?' They heard the man come into the compartment. 'Strewth, you've got enough clobber haven't you?' He kicked a kitbag.

'Go easy, mate. There's a secret weapon in there,' said one of the soldiers. 'What time d'you reckon we'll get to London?'

The ticket man snorted. 'Think of a time, and then add on two or three hours. There's so many extra trains, nobody knows where we are. Munitions, troops — anybody'd think there was a war on.' The men responded with good humour. 'Best of luck lads. Give 'em what for.'

'He's gone!'

The soldiers uncovered Alf and Audrey, and they emerged red-faced and panting for breath. They thanked the soldiers, one of whom opened the window.

'You two had better get some fresh air.'

They leaned out of the carriage window. So far their luck had held. They grinned at each other, as the fields sped by and the wind tugged at their hair.

Once Alf had told Audrey that he was going to see his dad, she begged to go with him. He hadn't been too sure about whether she should. She had said she was going to run away anyway, because she was

132

certain she was going to be put in a home. So he'd agreed. The most important thing was that he got to his dad in time. Nothing else mattered but that. Whatever trouble he and Audrey might end up in.

They went to the reference section of the local library to look at an atlas. They found what they wanted in the index: *Haywards Heath, England. P 23, 51.ON:0.5N.* With some help from the librarian, they located the town on the map. It was a good bit south of London and about fifteen miles from the coast. It looked a long way from Smethwick. Their plan was simple. To go to London and find their way from there. Alf had left a note for Granny Dugmore, and instead of going to school he and Audrey had gone to New Street Station in Birmingham.

Alf had one pound seven shillings left from his Uncle Bill's money, and Audrey had only one and tenpence. They realised they would need this for food and would have to risk travelling without tickets. Actually getting on the train had been easy. Two penny platform tickets had got them past the barrier and nobody had said anything when they had got on the train.

'I'll tell you something funny,' said one of the older soldiers. 'I've got a couple of kids, just about your age. But if I knew they were doing what *you* are doing, I'd belt them. Yet here we are, helping you to break the law. The funny thing is . . . I hope you get away with it!'

'Why are you going to London?' asked another, handing cigarettes round to his pals.

Just as Alf was about to answer, Audrey spoke. 'We are evacuees, but we've managed to escape.'

'*Escape*?'

Audrey nodded. 'We was stuck on this farm in the country, see. They didn't half mek us work. It was horrible. The woman give us next to nothing to eat. One time she only give us pig food for a week.

That was when she copped Alf trying to pinch the hens' eggs.'

The men looked at Alf. Amazed at Audrey, he had no choice but to carry on with her stupid story. 'It was because we were so hungry. But the trouble was, she'd-counted them. The eggs. Every one.' He turned to Audrey with a mischievous glint in his eye. 'And do you remember that time in the dairy?'

'Oh yes.' She nodded vigorously. And then asked, 'What happened?'

'It was a dark, frosty morning in winter. We were doing the milking. Audrey was milking Daisy. She was a nice cow usually, but that morning she was frisky and started playing up. Anyway, she kicked Audrey's pail of milk over. They locked her up for that.'

'The cow?' asked a soldier.

'No, Audrey.'

There was a brief silence. Somebody spoke. 'Where?'

All eyes turned on Audrey. 'In an old shed. There was cobwebs, and spiders. And mice.'

'No rats?' wondered a soldier.

'Now I come to think on it, there *might* have bin,' she replied. 'Any road, the one good thing was, there was a gap under the door. So Alf could push notes through to me.'

'Why didn't he speak to you instead?'

They all looked at Alf. But it was Audrey who went on. 'Because of *her*. If her'd copped him, her'd've banged him in the cellar. And I wouldn't have had nothing to eat.'

Alf continued. 'The gap was just big enough for me to slide a bit of toast through. I used to steal it when the farmer wasn't looking,'

'Didn't they count that as well?' asked one of the men, with a wink at the others.

The train, which had been slowing down, finally came to a halt. The soldiers gave a chorus of groans and examined the empty countryside.

'Where are we?' one of them asked.

'In the middle of nowhere,' someone replied.

They heard the chug and clanking of a goods train slowly draw up on the other line. It was carrying fighter planes, each one clearly marked with three broad white stripes on its fuselage and wings. Alf was told this was to assist identification during the invasion.

'Yank planes, aren't they?' said a voice.

'I reckon. Dunno what they are.' The soldier grinned. 'Hope they're up there when we land!'

'Forget it. They're never there when you want them.'

'And when they are, they usually end up bombing the wrong side.'

'What do you mean?' asked Alf.

'American pilots — got no experience. They get lost, and then they flap. So they just drop their load anywhere and buzz off.'

'My dad's going to be in the invasion,' he told them.

'Well, tell him to keep his tin hat on when the Yanks are around.'

The soldiers chuckled and Alf responded with a weak smile. They talked about the Americans like Uncle Bill. Nevertheless, he was glad they were on our side and silently prayed they would bomb the right places. However, just to be on the safe side, he would warn his dad.

Audrey tapped one of the men on the shoulder. 'D'you like being in the army?'

The men exploded with laughter. 'You're a right little comic, you are,' replied the soldier.

'I once met a bloke who liked it,' said the man sitting next to him. 'Mind you, he was drunk at the time, and he'd just banged his head on the cookhouse door.'

Once more the compartment rang with their laughter.

*   *   *

It was evening when the train eventually arrived at Euston Station. Every inch of the place was crowded and noisy. Steam hissed from the engines and between the carriages, and rose to form a smelly fog that seemed to cling to the yellow station lights. Servicemen and women with their kitbags jostled each other, as they tried to find a way through the mass of people. Unintelligible announcements boomed from loudspeakers and added to the confusion.

The soldiers had said they would get Alf and Audrey past the ticket barrier. But they had quickly been lost in the crowd and the two found themselves hemmed in a queue that was slowly moving towards the barrier.

'What we going to do?' asked Audrey, nervously clinging to Alf's arm.

'I'm not sure.' He put his hand into hs pocket and held on to his piece of lucky shrapnel.

'I in' half scared.'

Alf's reply was lost in the extra noise made by a line of mail trolleys being driven down the platform. Its horn blared and the people in the queue cursed as they were forced to make room for it. As the last trolley trundled by, Alf tugged Audrey and pointed. She got the idea and nodded. They ran after the trolley and jumped on. Quickly, they burrowed beneath the sacks of mail.

'Oo . . . they smell like dirty socks,' said Audrey.

'Ssh.'

They knew they were safely through the ticket barrier when their trolley started bumping over a different surface. Risking a look out, Alf saw they were heading for a loading bay. He helped Audrey get clear of the sacks and they jumped off.

'Hey, you!' A Post Office man had seen them. He shouted again.

Instinctively they ran back towards the station and pushed into the crowd. They followed the general movement until they saw a queue at the refreshment room.

'Let's get something to eat,' said Alf.

'That man might see us.'

'No he won't. Come on, I'm starving.'

After a long wait they each managed to get a cup of tea and a bun. They found a space and were glad to have a wall to lean against. A woman banged down a large suitcase beside them.

'Will you keep an eye on that for me?' They agreed. 'Ta.' She went off to queue at the counter and Alf and Audrey sat on her case.

'How we going to find out where to go?' asked Audrey.

'We'll ask somebody,' said Alf. 'We'll have to go to another station. I'm sure of that.' He remembered having to change trains in London with his parents.

'It's dark outside,' said Audrey.

'We'll be all right. We can go by Underground. Got your money safe?'

She nodded.

The woman came back and they stood up. She thanked them.

'Could you tell us the station for Haywards Heath, please?' Alf asked the woman.

'Oo . . . Victoria, I should think. It'll be Southern Region, won't it? Mind you, you'd better check.' She eyed them. 'By yourselves, are you?'

'We're waiting for my mom,' said Alf quickly.

'And don't *she* know?' asked the woman.

'Her forgot,' said Audrey.

'Fancy that,' replied the woman suspiciously.

Alf pointed and waved his arm across the room. 'Look — there she is!' He grasped Audrey's hand. 'Come on!' He pulled her after him, and set out to search for the nearest Underground sign.

Their journey to Victoria proved to be simple. They bought Underground tickets and then waited by the queue until they heard someone ask for the same station. By following the unsuspecting man, they arrived at the main line station. Victoria, like Euston, was also very crowded, and to their dismay they discovered that they had missed the last train to Haywards Heath. They wandered around the edge of the crowd. There were people sitting or sleeping on every available bench.

'Lookin' for somewhere to doss down?'

They were suddenly aware of a boy standing in front of them. He looked about fourteen and was smoking a cigarette.

'The cops'll nab you if you stop 'ere,' he went on. ''specially a couple o' kids like you.' He made a show of blowing smoke from his nostrils. 'They come round in the night.'

Audrey looked anxiously at Alf and took his hand.

'I know a place, see. They used to use it in the blitz. It's near 'ere. Dead 'andy. Warm and everythink. Cost you a bob.'

They nodded. As the boy had shrewdly expected, mention of the police had done the trick. He led them back towards the Underground. Beside the entrance there was an emergency exit, protected by a wall of sandbags. AIR RAID SHELTER said a large notice, and one or two weary travellers were already investigating its possibilities. The boy elbowed his way through.

'You don't want to stop up 'ere. You want to get down below where it's warm.'

They followed him down a long, dimly lit stair. At the bottom they turned into a passageway that led them to an unused platform. There were bunks along the wall, leaving a narrow gap between them and the edge of the platform.

'There you are,' said the boy. 'Beds an' all. That's a bob.'

Alf had all his money in a leather purse Grandad Charlie had once given him. He took it out and tried to find a shilling in the dim light. The next thing he knew, he was falling backwards into the darkness. The boy had pushed him and snatched his purse. Alf fell off the platform.

Audrey screamed and ran after the boy. He slipped on the dark stair and she managed to grab his coat. They wrestled on the stair. She scratched and kicked and he yelled in pain. When he was able to get to his feet, she hung on to him. One hand holding his hair, the other, an ear. He was in agony and jabbed his elbow into her side. As she let go and fell, he aimed a kick at her. She grabbed at his foot and felt herself propelled down the stair. He ran away upwards, swearing and snivelling.

Bruised and frightened, Audrey went quickly back to the platform. Alf was nowhere to be seen. She shouted his name. To her relief she saw his head appear over the edge of the platform. She helped him to climb up. Luckily he'd not fallen on the rails. These had been covered up with sandbags to prevent accidents. He was winded and had hurt his elbow.

They sat on a bunk, alone and afraid. The only money they had left was Audrey's one and tenpence.

'What's that?' Alf whispered, pointing to a dim object on the platform.

'His shoe,' said Audrey. 'I got hold of his foot.' In spite of their fear, Alf gave a laugh. 'I bit him an' all,' she added. 'He tasted horrible, the stinking pig.'

Alf rose unsteadily to his feet, his head aching.

'You all right?' she asked him.

'Just a bit dizzy,' he replied. He picked up the shoe and threw it as hard as he could into the darkness.

'I hope it's raining up there and he treads on a six-inch nail,' said Audrey, rubbing her sore ribs.

They spent the night huddled together and got a little sleep. It was just after six o'clock in the morning when they went back upstairs to the station. They knew they had to get some food. The refreshment room was closed, but they saw a crowd of soldiers at a mobile canteen. Joining them they waited their turn and sacrificed sevenpence on two cups of tea and a fishpaste sandwich. This was no sooner halved than it was eaten, leaving them still hungry. But they agreed they couldn't risk spending any more.

The train for Haywards Heath was not due to leave until half-past eight. They planned to use their platform ticket trick to get on it. In the meantime they found an unoccupied bench and prepared to wait, each trying to pretend they were not tired and hungry.

Alf dozed. He had a confused dream about his dad. He was running after him, but never seemed to reach him. Dave was singing and joking just as he had done in the act. There was a burst of applause. Alf awoke with a jolt. Strangely the applause continued. Realising where he was, he looked for Audrey. She wasn't beside him. Alarmed, he jumped up. He noticed that it was a crowd of American soldiers who were clapping and whistling. He heard someone shout out: 'Sing it again!' More voices took up the cry.

We're going to Hit Hit Hitler
Where it Hurt Hurt Hurts . . .

Audrey! He squirmed his way through the servicemen and there she was, performing for all she was worth. He felt too dazed to join in, and just watched as she skilfully handled the number. Afterwards he helped her collect money and candy from the generous audience.

'Who's he?' asked a soldier, indicating Alf.

'My manager,' replied Audrey, raising a laugh.

The large group of Americans dumped their kit down and proceeded to have breakfast. They opened a variety of tins and cartons, and invited Alf and Audrey to join them. Within moments they were eating peanut butter and crackers, followed by milk and tinned fruit. Audrey nudged Alf, and nodded towards a policeman who was approaching.

The constable surveyed the group. 'You can't stop 'ere.'

'Why not officer?' asked an American voice.

'Because it's a railway station.'

'Oh good. We're in the right place, fellers. You see, officer, we have to catch a train.'

'That's all very well, but . . .'

'Would you like some peaches?'

The policeman was taken aback. 'Well . . . I wouldn't say no.'

'That's what Hitler said when they asked if he was a screwball.'

Everyone laughed.

'Who are these two?' Alf and Audrey sat still as the constable pointed at them. Neither replied. Fortunately one of the Americans spoke up.

'They're in show business. Entertaining the troops.'

'That right?' asked the constable doubtfully. The two of them nodded in unison. 'Bit young, aren't you?' They shook their heads.

'Heck, officer, ain't you heard of Shirley Temple?'

'She was *younger* when she started,' added a voice.

'That's right,' confirmed another. 'And these kids have got talent. Believe me, I'm a big-shot from Hollywood, and I know what I'm talking about.' The rest of the group laughed and the constable allowed himself a smile.

'Oh well, thanks for the peaches,' he said. 'Just you two make sure you're not late for school.' He ambled off whistling.

Later, when the soldiers were getting ready to leave, Alf asked if any of them knew Haywards Heath. They said there were a number of American and British units based in and around the town. Many were under canvas and the feeling was they would

141

be leaving very soon. Alf's anxiety increased. They must not be too late.

'You two doing a show down there?' asked an American, lifting his kitbag onto his shoulder.

'Sure thing!' replied Audrey.

Audrey's singing had earned them almost two pounds. At Alf's insistence they had bought proper tickets for Haywards Heath. He didn't want to risk anything going wrong. However, once they were standing in the corridor of the crowded train, he began to feel queasy. His head was hot and he knew he was going to be sick. The train had not yet started, so he flung open the door and jumped onto the platform. He rushed across to the other side and vomited over the edge. He heard the guard's whistle and Audrey yelling at him to get back in. Doors slammed and steam hissed. Still groggy, he straightened up and saw that the train had started to move. He ran towards it in panic. By now the door Audrey was holding open was ahead. He ran beside the train, but he knew he didn't have the strength to jump on. Suddenly his feet were off the ground and he felt himself lifted up and into the train. His rescuer was a tall sailor, who placed him down and slammed the carriage door. He smiled at Alf and carried on down the corridor.

Alf was too weak to stand and Audrey managed to find a space for him to sit on some luggage at the end of the corridor.

'You all right now?'

He nodded. She offered him one of the candy bars they'd been given. He shook his head and looked out of the window. The bomb-damaged suburbs of south London were passing by. He noticed a group of boys playing on a bombsite. Just as he had done. They fired their guns, clutched their wounded bodies, and died with heroic gestures. They looked stupid. Didn't *they* have fathers who might be killed? Didn't they know what was going on? He felt the sickness at the back of his throat and quickly put his hand over his mouth. The moment passed and he rested his forehead against the cool glass.

'Look. Look there!'

He heard Audrey's voice. He must have dozed. They were in the country, passing fields that were full of army lorries and equipment. In one field there were what looked like large flat boats, stacked up on each other in piles.

'What d'you think them are?' asked Audrey.

'Maybe they're boats.'

'No, they're pontoons,' said a soldier standing beside Alf. 'To make bridges with. They're for the Pioneers. Them and the Engineers bung 'em across rivers and that. The Germans won't have left many bridges.'

'My dad's in the Pioneer Corps,' said Alf.

'Well, good luck to him,' said the soldier. 'I think I'd rather stick in the Infantry. At least we can shoot back.'

'What do you mean?' asked Alf, concerned.

'Stands to reason,' he replied. 'You've got your hands full when you're building a bridge. They could knock you off easy.'

Alf was glad to gulp the fresh air outside Haywards Heath station.

'You don't half look poorly,' said Audrey.

'It must have been that peanut butter.'

'I thought it was smashing. D'you want to have a sit-down?'

'No. We've got to get on.' He took out a piece of paper on which he'd written his dad's address. 4917238 DUGMORE D, PTE., B COY, 2ND BN PIONEER CORPS, HAYWARDS HEATH, SX.

They surveyed the people and traffic. There appeared to be servicemen and vehicles of every shape and size.

143

'Ask a soldier,' suggested Audrey. She pointed at one. 'Him.'

'Sorry mate,' replied an Australian voice to Alf's question.

They walked on a little way until they came to some shops.

'Let's try in here.'

'Pioneers?' repeated the shopkeeper. 'They're ours, aren't they? You know, British?' They nodded. 'Really, there's so many. American, Canadian, French . . . I tell you, I wouldn't be surprised if there weren't a few Germans amongst them!' She thought hard. 'Well, there's *definitely* a British camp down the Ditching road. Mind you, it's a longish way.'

'Are there any buses?' Alf asked her.

'Lord love you, there's not a hope of that. In fact, now I come to think of it . . .' She shouted through into the house. 'Frank, is it all right, the Ditching road? Or did they close that as well?' She listened to a mumbled reply. 'No, it's okay. It's the small roads off it that's closed. So I think you should try down there. Can't think of any of our boys anywhere else.'

They queued at a baker's on their way through the town. The women in front of them were listening to the latest invasions rumour from a red-faced man.

'That big American camp, down by Plumpton, it's empty. They've gone, I tell you.'

'What do you mean?'

'What you think I mean? They're not there. Moved out in the night.'

'D'you think it's started then?'

'Must have done.'

'Maybe they're just doing their training. You know, like they have been.'

'Then why did they take everything with them?' said the man knowingly.

Alf stepped out of the queue. 'Come on. We haven't got time.' He started to run and Audrey had difficulty

144

keeping up with him along the busy pavement. He didn't stop until the shops were far behind them. They were both panting and Audrey had a stitch.

'Hang on a bit, Alf.'

'You heard what they said. It could have started. The invasion.'

She held on to a garden fence to get her breath back. 'Well, if it *has*,' she panted, 'we'm too late anyway. And there's nothing we can do about it.'

Alf refused to see the sense of what Audrey was saying. 'Come on!' he shouted at her desperately.

She sat on the ground with her back against the fence. 'I've got to have a rest,' she said.

'Please . . .' he begged her. 'We can still get there if we hurry.'

'I can't hurry no more.'

'I've got to get to my dad,' he cried. 'You know I have.'

Tears filled Audrey's eyes and she shook her head wearily. 'Alf . . . I can't . . .'

A fierce frustration welled up in Alf. He was torn between his loyalty to Audrey and his anxiety to find his father. He was convinced that every wasted minute made it more likely that he would not be able to get to Dave in time. He said the only thing he could think of.

'You wait here. I'll go on. I'll come back for you . . .'

'No, Alf . . .'

'I will,' he told her. I promise . . .'

He left her and carried on down the road.

Audrey sobbed and felt hatred for Alf boiling up inside her. She'd helped him and been a good pal, and this was the thanks she got. Just like a boy. Only think of themselves. She'd show him. He wasn't going to treat her like that. She stood up. Her anger gave her strength. Wiping her face she strode down the road, determined to give Alf a piece of her mind.

It was a long, hard walk. Even when she reached the open countryside there was no sign of Alf. Could he have got a lift from one of the army vehicles using the road? The thought frightened her. She would be left completely on her own. She had passed small side roads. But these had been lined with stationary jeeps and trucks as far as the eye could see. He wouldn't have gone down one of them. This seemed to be another area for storing things ready for the invasion. Eventually she reached a lane that turned off to her left. A small temporary signpost said 2 BN PIONEERS. She went down the lane and started to run, sure she would find Alf now.

She did. He was half crouched, half lying at the side of the lane. He'd been sick again and was shivering. Audrey ran to him. As she tried to sit him up, there was an explosion. The noise and the surprise threw them together and they lay on the grass verge, both tense with fear. There was another explosion, farther away this time. Black smoke drifted over the hedges at the side of the lane. They waited, hardly daring to breathe.

After a few minutes' silence, they eased themselves up and looked around. There was nothing to be seen. Alf was deathly white. He continued to shiver and his face was damp with sweat.

'You'm ill,' whispered Audrey, full of concern.

He shook his head weakly. 'No, no, I'll be all right now you're here.' His voice was hoarse and he had difficulty in speaking.

'We can't stay here. I dunno what them bangs was, but I don't like them.' She stood up and peered down the lane. What she saw made her go weak with fear. 'Oh, my God.' A distant line of tanks was coming round a bend, heading towards them. They were enormous and brushed the hedgerows on either side of the lane. As they approached, the roar of engines

146

and clank of caterpillar tracks grew louder. Audrey pulled Alf to his feet.

'Quick, quick!' she shouted at him, and tugged him after her. They made slow progress because Alf was so weak. Terrified, Audrey saw the tanks approaching. She couldn't see any men in them. They were shut up. Blind, it seemed. But still they lumbered on. Alf was going slower. Frantically she screamed at him. Her voice was lost in the advancing din. She waved her arms at the leading tank in an attempt to stop it. But it didn't falter. It came on, its tracks crunching into the lane. She could feel the ground vibrating beneath her.

In absolute terror Audrey flung herself at Alf and they fell onto the grass verge. Desperately she scrambled at the hedge to find a way through. The branches slashed at her face, but she forced her body into the leaves and felt them give a little. She pushed harder and pulled Alf's body against her. Their combined weight had sufficient impact to force a way into the undergrowth. Even as Alf was still dragging himself through, the first tank went past. They felt the sudden violent heat of its exhaust and were smothered in choking fumes.

They crawled away from the hedge into the field and lay in the fresh green hay crop that was growing there. The rumble of the tanks was deafening and they felt the ground shaking. Neither moved after the last tank had gone. They lay numb with shock.

A bird singing brought Audrey to her senses. She listened, unbelieving. Then the sweet smell of the grass came to her. She roused herself, wincing with pain from the scratches on her hands and face. The sky was blue and, apart from the bird, it was still and silent again.

She heard a soft rasping sound. It was Alf's breathing. He too was badly scratched, but he appeared to be sleeping for the moment. She stood up, feeling stiff and tired. Audrey now knew for certain what she must do. She had to get help for Alf. He was ill and they must forget about trying to find his father. Her first thought was to get him to the main road and hope to wave down a car. Then she noticed they were quite close to a track that wound its way across the field. It went out of sight as the land got higher, so she ran along it to see what was on the other side. There was a farm. With a tremendous sigh of relief, she rushed back to Alf. Rousing him wasn't easy. By now he was snoring and she couldn't help smiling at him.

He woke up and with Audrey's help and encouragement managed to walk slowly beside her. As the track rose she pointed at the farm. He focused his eyes and nodded. He too had accepted that they couldn't go on searching for his dad.

The farm was unnaturally quiet. When they reached the first out-buildings there were no signs of animals, people, or even farm machinery. The whole place appeared to be deserted. They went up to the farmhouse. When Audrey knocked on the door it swung open. At the same moment there was a crash from inside and a large rat streaked past her into the yard. She screamed and leapt aside, as she felt it brush her leg. She clung on to Alf and they waited. Silence returned.

Cautiously they made their way in. There was still some furniture and even a little food left in the cupboards. And the tap worked. They sat down at the kitchen table and gratefully drank some water.

'Oo, Alf — look!' Audrey pointed at a telephone on the sideboard. 'We can phone somebody up.' She would have preferred him to do it, but he would have difficulty in speaking. She picked up the receiver.

'What shall I do?'

'The operator,' Alf croaked, using all the effort he could muster. 'Dial 0.'

She dialled carefully and listened. 'I can't hear

nothink.' She dialled again. 'Here, listen.' She handed
Alf the receiver.

'It's dead.'

'What?'

'It's been cut off.'

'Why they done that?'

He gestured weakly. 'Nobody here.'

They would have to walk back to the main road.
Audrey groaned. It was now farther than ever away.
She went through her pockets. They would at least
have something to eat before they set off. She still had
a few packets of gum and a Babe Ruth bar left from
what the Americans had given them.

Alf felt hungry, but the last thing he wanted to do
was swallow anything. His throat was sore and he
even had difficulty with the water. He nibbled his
half of the chocolate bar and his eyes watered with
pain as he tried to swallow. The taste reminded him
of Christmas. Of Lee and his mom. A time when
everything had been smashing. Or had it . . .? What
about his dad? The thought of his selfishness and
stupidity made him feel sick again.

'Come on.' Audrey was wiping his face with a damp
cloth. 'We better get off.'

They left the house and crossed the farmyard. There
were a series of brilliant flashes, quickly followed by
explosions. They halted in panic. Immediately there
came the crack of small arms fire and the stutter of
a bren-gun. As fast as they could, Alf and Audrey
got back into the house and slammed the door
behind them. The noise continued and they realised
they were surrounded by some sort of battle. They
went upstairs to one of the bedrooms. From there
they could see earth and debris thrown up by the
explosions. Audrey remembered what the woman in
the queue had said about troops training. This is
what must be happening. She turned to tell Alf and
found him lying on the bed shivering. There were no

bedclothes, so she covered him up with an old rug from the floor.

Audrey knew that she had to get help for Alf and the only hope of that was to make contact with the soldiers training in the fields outside. She left the farmhouse with a feeling of mounting terror. The crackle of rifle fire and the thump of exploding mortar shells seemed even louder than before. A vile-smelling smoke drifted across the farmyard like a fog, as she forced herself to find the track she and Alf had used to get to the farm. She kept close to the wall of a barn for shelter, and then, just as she turned round the corner of the building, she tripped over a body and fell to the ground with a scream.

'What the blazes are you doing here?' asked the soldier, but Audrey was too shocked to reply. 'Don't mind me — I'm dead,' he went on. 'About time too. I was needing a rest. All this pretending takes it out on you.' He studied Audrey as she stood up. 'But you shouldn't be here. You could get hurt.'

'Are you in the Pioneers?' Audrey asked him abruptly.

'Blimey!' exclaimed the soldier. 'You a spy or something?'

'Me friend's poorly, and we'm looking for his dad. He's in the Pioneers. They'm down here somewhere.'

'That's right. They're on this exercise,' he said. 'I'm Engineers myself. Sorry.'

'His name's Dave Dugmore . . .'

'Hold on,' said the soldier. 'That rings a bell. That was the name of a bloke who done a turn at the camp concert . . . used to be on the halls . . .'

'That's him!' Audrey cried. 'Mister, could you take me to him?'

'Strewth, that's asking a bit — I'm supposed to be dead.'

'But you're not really,' said Audrey, taking hold of

his arm and trying to pull him up. 'Come on — it's urgent. I can't find him by myself in the middle of this lot'

'Well . . . I might be able to track down his unit,' said the soldier reluctantly. 'But . . .'

'That'll do,' said Audrey. 'Come on . . .'

Alf lay with his eyes closed. He was aware of the noise from outside, but it seemed to come and go in waves. Incredibly, when his teeth chattered, he wasn't able to hear anything else at all, not even the explosions. Biting his teeth to keep them still made his throat feel worse. He was sure it was now red raw. He couldn't understand what he'd done to be made to suffer like this. Was it because he'd run away? His mind became a mad kaleidoscope of impressions. Everywhere he'd ever been; everyone he'd ever known; they all wanted to appear. He couldn't stop them. His gran, Mrs Kenrick, people he'd known on the halls and forgotten about. His mom singing; his dad seeing the policeman. Dot, Lee, his Uncle Bill and Amy, all fought to get his attention. He tried to shout at them. To tell them to go away. But he had no voice. The boy who had stolen his money thought that was very funny. He laughed at him. Alf tried to punch him to kick him. But he dodged away, still laughing.

He woke up writhing on the bed. His throat was on fire. After a moment he realised there was no sound from outside. He looked for Audrey and found she wasn't there. It was dusk and the room was dark. He wanted to cry. But no tears came. As though the pain would not allow him the relief of crying. Even now that he was awake, his mind's eye held on to the crazy images of his dream. The tanks, the woman in the shop, the soldiers on the train. They wouldn't leave him. Then he heard singing. The soldiers. The sound got louder . . . He knew what it was. They were singing 'Lili Marlene'.

He forced himself up off the bed. The singing continued, and he realised it was coming from outside. He hung on to the window-sill and could now hear marching feet as well. He looked out of the window and could just make out a squad of soldiers coming up the lane. There was something odd about them. As they got closer he could see what it was. They were Germans! He recognised the unmistakable shape of their helmets. Two figures broke away from the group and hurried ahead. One of them was a girl. Audrey! They must have taken her prisoner and she was trying to escape. The other one was a German soldier. Their feet clattered as they ran into the farmyard. The front door banged and he heard the soldier come up the stairs and burst into his room.

Alf stared at the enemy uniform and blackened face. He tried to shout, but produced only a stab of pain, causing him to stagger. Strong arms caught him and laid him on the bed.

The soldier took off his helmet and spoke.

'Hullo son,' said Dave.

10

Alf opened his eyes and saw three white-gowned figures standing at the foot of his bed. They wore masks over their faces. His eyes hurt, so he closed them and listened to their voices.

'You must have heard of immunisation? Good heavens, there's been enough publicity in the papers and on the wireless.'

'We've moved about a lot . . .' said a man who sounded like his dad.

'We've been inoculating against diphtheria since 1940 — four years. Don't you realise what you were risking for your son?'

'. . . we do now, doctor.' It was a woman. His mom — it had to be!

Alf tried to sit up, but he couldn't move. And it seemed he couldn't even open his eyes again. Inside himself he shouted to them. But he knew they didn't hear him because he hadn't made a sound. It was like he was being tortured.

However, he felt a moment's relief before he fell asleep. It came from a cool hand placed on his brow and the smell of his mother's scent.

It was still there when he woke up. This time he felt much better and he recognised his mother and father, even though they were still wearing gowns and masks. 'Why have you got those things on?' he whispered.

Dave answered. 'You're infectious, mate. That's why you're in a room by yourself. You've been and gone and got diphtheria.'

153

'Don't worry,' said Sonia. 'You'll soon be well again.'

'Where are we?' Alf asked them.

'In London,' Sonia told him. 'They brought you here, after dad found you.'

Dave sat on the side of Alf's bed. 'Do you remember the explosions and the shooting?' Alf nodded. 'Well, it was a training exercise. My company were supposed to be Germans and the Americans were attacking us. Audrey left you in the farmhouse to go and get help. The poor thing, she just about collapsed when she came across us all dressed up.'

'Where is Audrey?'

'I got some digs,' said his mother. 'She's there. They won't allow her in to see you because of the risk of infection.'

'But she wrote you a letter,' said Dave, reaching into a pocket under his gown.

Sonia helped Alf to sit up and he read the letter.

Dear Alf,

I hope you are getting better. They kep me in hospital as well for a bit in case I get diptheria like you. I was all right but they told me poor Harry died on it. It made me cry. Your mom is looking after me. My moms gone of and when I get back to Smethwick I'm going to be put in an home. Send us a letter.

love
Audrey.

He looked at his parents. 'Her brother died?'

They nodded and Sonia took his hand.

'Mom, *will* they put her in a home?'

'I'm not sure what will happen,' his mother replied. 'We'll have to wait and see. The Council have said I can look after her in the meantime. But I've had to agree to take her back.'

Dave cleared his throat and put on a cheery voice. 'This came for you.' He gave Alf a small parcel.

It was a bag of barley sugar sweets from Granny Dugmore and Grandad Charlie. Alf looked at the sweets. The meaning of what he had done and why he had run away came back to him. His throat started to throb and as he started to speak, all that came out was a sob. He couldn't look at his parents and he began to cry as they put their arms around him.

Alf was in hospital for three weeks and as he got better he replied to the notes his mother brought him from Audrey. She had been in heaven, living with her 'dream mom', but that had had to end. The time soon came when Sonia had to take her back to Smethwick and Alf was left feeling thoroughly wretched. Once again it seemed he'd got everything, and she was going to end up stuck in a children's home. He could not shake off the belief that it was all his fault, even on the day Dave came to get him from the hospital.

As they left the building, the steps outside were crowded with people watching wave after wave of planes flying overhead. All the aircraft had three white stripes on each wing, and some of the nurses claimed they could see the pilots waving back at them.

'Does that mean the invasion's started?' Alf asked Dave.

'Yes,' replied his father.

The streets were full of small groups of people watching and waving. Alf noticed passengers jumping off a bus to get a better view. And a bunch of taxi drivers had abandoned their cabs and were drinking and shouting outside a pub. 'Give 'em what for lads! Go and knock old Hitler for six!'

Alf looked at his dad and they smiled.

When they got to the digs, Alf noticed Audrey's wellington boots in a corner. His heart skipped a beat. Maybe she hadn't gone? But he knew Sonia had taken her back to Smethwick several days ago and was due to return that day.

Dave saw what he was thinking. 'Mom got Audrey some shoes. And she fixed her up with a new dress.'

Alf nodded and went to the window and watched the planes. After a moment his father spoke to him.

'Alf, I've got to go back tomorrow. My compassionate leave ran out last week, but the CO let me have a thirty-six hour pass to come and collect you from the hospital.'

'Does that mean you've missed the invasion?' Alf asked.

Dave smiled. 'The first bit, maybe. But I'll soon be joining in. Anyway, I want you to know, I'm not cross with you for running off like you did. I should be mad at you, but... I'm glad you wanted to see me. I can't tell you how much that means to me.' Alf turned to face him. 'Are we mates now?'

Alf nodded his head. The memory of what he'd thought about his father made him squirm. How could he have done that? His dad was smashing.

Sonia arrived in the afternoon, full of smiles as she hugged Alf. She had brought him clothes from Granny Dugmore's and a new leather purse with a shilling in it from Grandad Charlie.

'Well, aren't you going to ask me how we got on?' she asked him brightly.

Alf remained silent. His guilty conscience was still pricking him about Audrey and he couldn't bear to hear what had happened to her in Smethwick. And he didn't want his mother to start trying to cheer him up about it either.

'I'm going out to look at the planes,' he told his mother and father.

'Don't you want to hear about Audrey?' Sonia asked him.

He shook his head and ran out of the door. His mother called and went after him. 'Alf — it's going to be all right. Audrey's not going to be put in a home. She's going to live with Dot.'

Alf looked at her in disbelief and she led him back into the room.

Sonia went on. 'Yes, it's true. Dot has been approved as a suitable foster parent for her. Dad and me got the idea when Audrey told us how much she'd enjoyed rehearsing with you in your room. I didn't say anything to you in case it didn't come off. But Dot was happy to do it and the Council agreed. So, that means she'll be looking after Audrey.'

His mother stopped speaking and waited for Alf to say something. But he remained silent. He put his hand in his pocket and felt his lucky shrapnel. For once in her life, good luck had gone Audrey's way. And it wasn't just ordinary good luck — it was brilliant good luck.

'Aren't you pleased for Audrey?' asked Sonia.

He nodded. And nodded again. And then he found he was laughing for all he was worth and his throat was not a bit sore.

'Hold on! You're supposed to be an invalid!' cried Dave with a huge grin. 'I promised the doctor you wouldn't overdo things.'

'What did Dot say?' Alf asked when he had got his breath back.

'She said it would be a nice change to have a real girl as Cinderella next Christmas,' Sonia told him. 'She also said they would fit you in as Buttons — if you are free.'

Alf grinned. He was still having difficulty believing it was all true and really happening.

Sonia went on. 'And Audrey says you're welcome to drop in for a bit of toast any time you like.'

The three of them laughed at this remark and as their laughter died away, they stood smiling at each other. Alf was the first to speak.

'What about *us*?' he asked his parents.

Sonia glanced at her husband and then sat down. 'In a roundabout way, Audrey helped *me*, Dave.' She spoke to Alf. 'When you were in hospital, I taught her one or two routines. She enjoyed it — and so did I. We had a good time and it gave me an idea. I know what I'm going to do now.'

Alf saw his father's face become serious as he listened to Sonia's decision.

She smiled at them. 'I'm going to become a teacher. Oh, not like Mrs Kenrick,' she added when she saw their reaction. 'No, I'll teach singing and dancing for the stage. For youngsters . . .'

'Like Audrey,' said Alf.

'That's right,' agreed Sonia. 'Though to tell you the truth, she doesn't need much teaching. She's a natural. It's just as well we had *you* in our act Alf, and not her — she'd have taken over! Anyway, Audrey's one in a million. I'm sure there are lots of proud mothers who would like their children to perform. How does the Sonia Dugmore Stage School sound to you?'

Alf looked at his father. Dave's expression had now relaxed into a fond smile.

'Great!' said father and son together.

'So you see,' Sonia went on, 'doing that, I'll also be able to look after Sonny here.' She ruffled Alf's hair.

'Where will it be mom — your school?' asked Alf.

'In Birmingham.'

'But where will we live?'

'In Grandad Charlie's house,' she told him. 'You know it was bombed?' They nodded. 'Well it's been repaired, but he doesn't want to move back now. He and Granny Dugmore have got used to each other's company. So . . . he's going to rent it to us.' She paused and caught Dave's eyes. 'You, me, and dad. Just as we always used to be,' she added, taking her husband's hand.

Alf remembered how he used to be embarrassed when his parents kissed each other. However as they kissed each other now, he didn't feel himself go red, he just felt happy.

He went to the window and watched yet another flight of planes high in the sky.

Of course he knew his father would have to go back. All the wishing in the world wouldn't alter that. But they were a family again. They would be like loads of other families throughout the country. Living in hope and love until the war was over.